Jerry B. Jenkins is a prolific novelist and biographer whose writing has appeared in *Reader's Digest, The Saturday Evening Post,* the *Chicago Tribune,* and dozens of Christian periodicals. His *Out of the Blue* (with Orel Hershiser) reached the *New York Times* best-seller list. He is Writer-in-Residence at the Moody Bible Institute of Chicago and lives with his wife and boys at Three Son Acres, west of Zion, Illinois.

THE Deacon's Woman AND OTHER PORTRAITS

THE *Deacon's Woman* AND OTHER PORTRAITS

Fiction by
Jerry B. Jenkins

MOODY PRESS
CHICAGO

ISBN: 0-8024-1738-8

1 2 3 4 5 6 7 8 Printing/AF/Year 96 95 94 93 92

Printed in the United States of America

To Dianna, my one and only

Among other books by Jerry B. Jenkins

Adult Fiction
    Rookie
    The Operative
    The Margo Mysteries
    The Jennifer Grey Mysteries

Children's Fiction
    Dallas O'Neil and the Baker Street Sports Club
    The Dallas O'Neil Mysteries
    The Tara Chadwick Series
    The Bradford Family Adventures

Nonfiction
    Fourth and One (with Joe Gibbs)
    Singletary on Singletary (with Mike Singletary)
    Out of the Blue (with Orel Hershiser)
    Hedges: Loving Your Marriage Enough to Protect It
    Hymns for Personal Devotions
    Twelve Things I Want My Kids to Remember Forever
    Meadowlark (with Meadlowlark Lemon)
    Rekindled (with Pat and Jill Williams)
    Sweetness (with Walter Payton)
    Bad Henry (with Hank Aaron)

CONTENTS

1. Portrait One—The Deacon's Woman   9
2. Portrait Two—Ditched   23
3. Portrait Three—Night Stranger   39
4. Portrait Four—A Midnight Clear   55
5. Portrait Five—Rich Man, Poor Man   73
6. Portrait Six—Mr. Ministry   91
7. Portrait Seven—The Almighty Deal   109
8. Portrait Eight—The Spurious Paramour   125
9. Portrait Nine—Truth and Time   143
10. Portrait Ten—The Tangled Web   163

First Suburban Church dominates a corner not far from where you live. Its members come from all walks of life and represent various levels of devotion and commitment, from the pure and selfless to the struggling and phony.

Though any seeming portrayal of actual persons, living or dead or undecided, is purely coincidental, resemblance to people you know is intentional. . . .

THE DEACON'S WOMAN

Margaret sat at her husband's funeral with his terrible secret in her purse.

Pastor Nigel Ingle looked directly at her and told five hundred First Suburban Church guests that Clinton was the most devout layman he had known in thirty years of ministry. In Margaret's peripheral vision, people nodded solemnly. Had it not been for what she had found in her husband's wallet, she too would have agreed.

Clinton had been killed in the prime of his life. With two daughters grown and gone and a son, Joey, a senior in high school, Clinton and Margaret were enjoying a freedom they had looked forward to for years.

Every few days that fall, they had enjoyed watching their son play soccer late in the afternoon. The previous Monday as was her custom, Margaret had set a folded blanket next to her in the stands to save a seat for her husband. He would join her near the end of the first quarter after having returned home from the office and changing out of his suit. They never missed a game and usually went out to eat with Joey afterward.

Margaret neither understood nor wholly enjoyed soccer, except for watching her son. The teams raced up and down the field in what seemed a madcap effort to eke out any kind of a score, and Margaret found herself looking at her watch, wondering if Clinton had been delayed. She hoped he'd found the book she bought for him that morning. It was a rare find. She was proud of herself.

Remaining items from the community-wide garage sale had been offered at the leisure center. Margaret couldn't imagine having missed anything at the sale, but a pro like she didn't take chances. She discovered an old biography of Babe Ruth she knew Clint would love, and she offered half the asking price of a dollar. The elderly woman running the sale said she was sure the owners would be glad to take anything for a leftover.

Margaret had left the fifty-cent gift on the desk in Clint's den. It would be just like him, she thought, to get started on it and be later than usual to the game. One of the things he appreciated most about her, he'd always insisted, was her selection of gifts. "An inexpensive but personally appropriate gift is much more meaningful than something expensive but impersonal."

Joey fed a pass to the center forward that resulted in an early 1-0 lead. Margaret couldn't wait to tell Clint. But who was that with the police officer at the bottom of the stadium steps? What was Susan doing here?

Susan was Margaret's neighbor. The officer whispered something to her and discreetly stepped out of view. The crowd's attention, all but Margaret's, shifted back to the game. Her mind whirred. Was it one of the girls? Clint? It suddenly became clear. The officer didn't want a scene, but he had bad news. Much as she wanted to leap from her seat and confront Susan, she couldn't. The pain was etched deep on Susan's face.

Margaret looked pleadingly at her as she approached. Susan moved the blanket and sat, wrapping an arm around Margaret's shoulders. She drew her close and Margaret stiffened. She appreciated her friend's caring touch, but she knew this would be something she did not want to hear.

"Maggie, Clint's been in an accident. They came to your house, and I told them where you were. You need to come now."

Margaret stared straight ahead. Why had they felt it necessary to bring her neighbor? "Is he alive?"

"I don't know the details. A policeman is here—"

Margaret turned and stared deep into her friend's eyes. "Susan, don't make me hear it from a stranger. Please."

Susan embraced her and whispered, "Maggie, Clint was killed."

Margaret didn't hear the "I'm sorry" that Susan added. She felt her friend lift her and guide her down the steps.

"She made me tell her," Susan told the officer.

"I need to be back here at the end of the game," Margaret said. "I want to tell Joey myself."

The next hour was filled with questions and information. Margaret, in a mental fog, saw the twisted cars, heard what had happened, and was not surprised to hear it had not been Clinton's fault. He was such a careful driver. Her mind reeled with Scripture, prayer, details of the accident, seeing her husband of twenty-six years one more time, his color all wrong, a portion of his head carefully concealed.

She knew Clinton was in heaven. She would have been hard pressed to think of a character flaw. The same gentle, wise, friendly demeanor that made him a leader in his business and in the church also made him a wonderful father and husband. They didn't agree on everything, and he could be stubborn and impatient at times, but he was such a better person than she—she knew that without qualification.

Clinton was generous, others-oriented, consistent in his private worship and devotions. He was even a soul-winner, having been trained, taught an adult elective in personal evangelism, and even headed one of First Church's door-to-door witnessing teams. That was not for her. She shared her faith with her friends, but that cold approach to strangers—well, she admired Clinton and anyone else who could do it. She had faded quickly from that program.

Clint had been her life, her spiritual model and guide. She had been smug about her kids having never given them problems as most other adolescents did their parents. She knew Clint was the key. He was chairman of the deacons, respected, admired, and loved by everyone—even his own kids.

She could not cry. Not yet. She didn't know why. Part of her wanted to scream, to wake up, to back up a day and start over. But she had never been one to question God. In fact, she had always felt guilty that she and her family were so blessed. Others suffered, but she and Clint sailed merrily through life. He had to be the reason. She certainly didn't deserve such a life; in fact, if she got what she deserved, she thought, she would have lost a child or her husband long ago. She hadn't been evil. She just knew she had never taken enough risks or put herself out enough for the kingdom. Clint was always doing things like that. It was as natural to him as breathing.

How good he had been to her, and how she loved him!

At the morgue she was given a large manila envelope labeled "personal effects." She knew the stuff in that envelope would be too painful to deal with just now. Maps, napkins, and tapes from the glove compartment were one thing, but to see those personal items, the ones he put atop the dresser every night, no, she was not ready.

Telling her son and calling her daughters were her worst tasks ever. She sensed they knew before she sobbed out the words, and she was relieved, at last, to be able to cry.

Church friends spent the night with her and Joey and stayed the next morning until her daughters arrived. When she and the children were together she could not stop crying. They busied themselves with insurance policies and funeral arrangements. Clint had been typically thoughtful and thorough. She found everything in order.

The night before the funeral, Margaret wrote her simple portion of the eulogy and had it delivered to Pastor Ingle. She would be unable to speak, but he could read it. After a brief thanks for everyone's presence, calls, help, prayer, and other expressions of love, she wrote, "I want you all to know that Clinton was everything he appeared to be and more. He was truly a Christ-centered man from the inside out. Take it from one who knows."

Late that night before the funeral, Margaret could not sleep.

In the wee hours of the morning she sat alone in the kitchen in her robe, grateful for a lifetime in church, grateful for a bedrock joy and the confidence she felt that people cared and were praying for and loving her. Heaven seemed more real and closer than ever. She had imagined this day more than once and wondered how she would react. She was stunned at how painful was the blow, probably, she assumed, due to its suddenness. Life had kicked her in the stomach and left her gasping. She was thankful she would have no financial worries, but that was the least of her priorities. Clinton had been wrenched from her, as if amputated from her before she could even be sedated for the surgery.

At 2:00 A.M. she longed for rest but knew sleep would not come. Memories flooded her, and occasionally a wave of terror rolled over her. *What will I do without him?*

Margaret busied herself heating milk for hot chocolate, then pulled the manila envelope from atop the refrigerator. She was far enough from the bedrooms that no one would hear, but she fought a fear that someone would walk in on her in this most private moment. The crackling envelope was so loud that she put it in her lap and tore it open under the table.

She removed the contents one at a time. Clearly the glove box junk had gone in last, because it came out first. Nothing personal there except Clint's favorite Christian music tapes. She would have a selection played at the funeral, and then she would not listen to them for a long time.

When she reached the end of the impersonal stuff, his half-gone roll of breath mints slid from the envelope. Without thinking she popped one in her mouth. The sudden smell and taste of her husband made her shudder. She wanted to remove the mint and gulp her hot chocolate, but she could not. How sweet and painful was that flavor!

Keys, two receipts, and some change were next. Then came the wallet. Clinton's minty essence was in her mouth, making it seem as if he were with her. Margaret's hands shook as she browsed through his credit cards, business cards, and family pictures. She carefully replaced each in its sleeve; he would have appreciated that.

Behind the plastic photo insert and in front of his driver's license were six snapshots, placed loose in the wallet. The first was a picture of a dog she did not recognize. She stared at it a long time, knowing the other photos would probably answer the puzzle. She looked at the unfamiliar floor in the photo, the rug, the walls, the window, the unknown dog. The other five photos gave no clue. They merely stopped her heart and smashed it to pieces.

There in her husband's wallet, among the private personal effects of the only man she had ever loved, were photographs that could not be explained. She was not aware of her breathing or her pulse. She was aware of nothing but those pictures. She fanned them like a hand of cards, then looked at them one at a time.

Snapshots, that's all they were. Plain, simple, amateurish pictures taken with a modest camera. They evidenced a humble home of a lower middle-income family. Except for the dog, the pictures were of a woman.

She appeared to be in her mid- to late twenties, medium to tall, maybe ten pounds overweight with an attractive, athletic build. The woman had been photographed in a short, revealing negligee, and though her expression was one of slight embarrassment or bemusement, she had struck a variety of what Margaret could describe only as cheesecake poses: standing with her hands behind her head, sitting, legs crossed, negligee riding on her thighs, lying seductively on a water bed.

There was something sweet and innocent about the girl, despite the poses. Though Margaret held the breath mint in her teeth and felt her lifetime image of her husband swirling down a bottomless drain, she studied the photos for every detail.

Why did she feel a twinge of sympathy for this girl? Why did it appear, tacky and tawdry as these pictures were, that she had posed lovingly and willingly and yet not comfortably like some cheap sex object who would have done the same for anyone? If anything, the private nature of these photos, the obvious personal favor they had been from a young woman to her lover, made Margaret only more wretched.

She and Clint had responded, she felt, with appropriate maturity when they found a men's magazine in Joey's room a few years before. It would have hurt her deeply to find something similar in Clint's effects, but this . . . this shattered her. These were not mass-produced objects of voyeurism. These were the real thing, pictures of a living, breathing woman who had acquiesced to please her lover. This was clearly her husband, the deacon's, woman.

Margaret removed from her mouth what was left of the mint and dropped it into the now cold chocolate. Her head throbbed, and her breath came in short bursts. She turned the pictures over and discovered on the back of one: "C., with love and thanks for everything forever. Elaine."

So she had a name, this person twenty years younger than Margaret, this someone with youth and a firm body. Why did she feel she had to compete with this Elaine, even now with her husband just hours from his grave?

Margaret put the photos in the pocket of her robe and stood, steadying herself with a hand on the table. Though she had told herself it might be months before she could enter Clint's den, she now riffled through his files with abandon. The used book she had bought him lay on the corner of his desk where she had left it.

Finding no more evidence of Elaine, she pulled a plain, white envelope from a drawer and placed the pictures in it. In her grief and remorse and shock, she weighed this scandal against her lifetime of marriage and knew she must never let anyone see those pictures. She wondered whether she was being loyal to a man who had not been loyal to her, or merely protecting her own reputation.

Grief and anger and humiliation washed over her with such force she hardly knew whether to stand or sit, stay or leave, scream or weep. She startled herself by slamming the door as she left the den, wondering if her family would awaken and worry about her. No one stirred. She tidied up the kitchen, staring long and hard at the mints. She had an urge to melt them under the hot water tap, but she just wrapped the package tightly, opened the cabinet, and tossed it toward the waste basket under the sink. It missed, and she heard it hit and roll. She was in no mood to retrieve it.

Margaret trudged up to bed and lay on her back, amazed that she felt weary enough to doze. She folded her hands across her stomach, as she assumed Clinton was reposed, felt the envelope in her pocket, and wondered whether her friends and family would forgive her if she killed herself.

At First Suburban late the next morning she pulled Pastor Ingle aside. Before she could speak he asked if she'd gotten any sleep.

"I look that bad, do I?"

"You look tired, Margaret. You must lie down this afternoon. Everyone will understand."

"I would never be able to sleep."

"Simply resting will be helpful. Promise me."

"Pastor, I wanted to tell you I'd changed my mind about my tribute."

"You need to add something?" He reached into his breast pocket.

"No. I don't want you to read it after all."

"Margaret, I know it will be painful, but you've put it so well. It adds that personal—"

"I'd really rather you not."

"Whatever you say, but I must tell you, I couldn't have said it better."

Now Margaret sat in turmoil, her grief interrupted by such feelings of betrayal that she wondered if she could keep this horrible secret. All the wonderful things the pastor said and read about her husband would have seemed so true and right and comforting just a day before! Now they whiplashed her. Every expression by every friend and associate and relative included accolades of which no one was worthy. But they didn't know. How could they know?

In the ensuing days, when the unrelenting fingers of grief clutched her in the night, when she was more alone than she had ever been, she raged at God. How could this be? How could this have happened? She would have been happier to have been fooled, tricked, swindled, blissful in her ignorance. It would have been all right, she wailed aloud, to have buried an impostor, "if only I hadn't had to know!"

In her spiritual devastation and desperation, Margaret realized how fully she had hidden behind her husband. She had been taught it was biblical to be under his spiritual headship, yet he had always encouraged her to develop her own walk with God, her own time in the Scriptures. He wanted to see her grow and find a daily relationship with Christ that would carry her, "even if I'm no longer here."

She thought he had been referring to preceding her in death. Silly her. Crazy, trusting, believing, naive Maggie. She hadn't allowed him to discuss dying first. That was too much to fathom. Had she only known the unfathomable depths of the man!

Margaret was ill. She lost weight, lost color, her hair thinned. She didn't eat well or smart. She was frantic and felt trapped. She could tell no one. Much as she pleaded with God to show her how such a wonderful man could have been such a phony, it seemed heaven was silent. Soon she missed what little connection she'd had with God even more than she missed what had appeared an idyllic marriage.

If I don't do something, I'm going to fall apart, she decided. There would be, could be no answer to the greatest enigma in her life. For a few days she had told herself it all had to be a mistake, a misunderstanding. Maybe Clint had found those pictures in their son's room. But Joey was too young for a woman like that.

She could not push from her mind that the evidence was stark and unforgiving. There was no other explanation. Clinton had a younger woman on the side, and she was exciting to him. Would Margaret have posed for such pictures? Clinton would never have asked. Yet apparently he had asked someone else. Had Elaine been at the funeral? Margaret had not had the nerve to search the sea of faces for her.

Margaret did not blame God. She blamed Clinton. She searched her mind for memories of when he might have been less than honest with her, less than devoted, when he might have had opportunities to indulge himself. She knew she was reaching, exaggerating, making more out of conversations and comments than had really been there. Only when she quit working at it and pushed it from her mind did she get an iota of relief. And the only time she could accomplish that was when she sought God.

How ironic, she thought, as she sat in Clinton's chair, in Clinton's den, reading Clinton's well-used and well-marked Bible, that it was this ugly discovery that had pushed her to seek God on her own. She had been a Christian from childhood, and she had been active in her faith and worship. But she had been no Clint. Now her discovery of the real man behind the big Bible had spurred her to a daily devotional life Clint had always said he wanted for her.

Late one afternoon, as she pored over the Psalms, she heard a hesitant knock. It was her son. He seemed awkward and embarrassed.

"I'm worried about you, Mom," he said. "It's like you're mad at Dad or something. I feel bad too, but don't blame him."

She swallowed and nodded. She could not, would not ever tell him.

"I'm leaning on God," she said. "I've got a long way to go. You still reading your Bible every day?"

"'Course. Dad would be proud of me."

Don't say anything, she told herself. Not a word.

"What's this?" he said suddenly, noticing the Babe Ruth biography. "Where'd you get this?"

"Just a gift for you father."

"Did you see the ad?"

"The ad?"

"In the paper. It's all around school. Somebody sold one of these at the community garage sale, and now they want it back. They'll pay something like ten bucks for it, and they only sold it for a dollar."

"Fifty cents," Margaret said.

"That's where you got it? Mom! It's probably worth a lot of money! Why else would they want it back?"

"I don't know," she said. "It's yours if you want it."

"You mind if I sell it back to them?"

She shrugged. "Just don't get taken. Find out if it's worth more than what they're offering."

"I will!"

The next day Joey told her he had checked at a couple of secondhand stores. "It's worthless. I think I'll call the guy and get the ten bucks."

The following day Margaret received a call late in the afternoon from a man who had to shout over factory noise in the background. "Ma'am," he yelled, "are you the one who bought the Babe Ruth book?"

What now? she wondered. Joey had said it was worthless. "Yes."

"Did you find anything in it?"

"I didn't look in it."

"Your son tells me you bought it for your husband who has since passed away."

"That's right."

"I'm sorry!"

"Thank you."

"Ma'am, I need to talk to you. Could I visit you tonight?"

Her son would be home. And she was much too mature to be swindled. "I suppose. What about?"

"Well, it's personal and kinda embarrassing, so if you don't mind, I wouldn't take much of your time."

Margaret was nervous after dinner, waiting and wondering. At seven she opened the door to a husky young man with longish blond hair, a black T-shirt, jeans, and boots.

"Sorry to bother you, ma'am," he said, sitting heavily on the sofa. "I paid your son the ten bucks like I said I would, but my wife and me were really kinda hopin' you'd found somethin' in my book."

"Like what?"

He shrugged and smiled and looked at the floor. "Well, pictures actually."

"Pictures of what?"

He looked at her and looked away. "Well, uh, my dog. My dog and, uh, my wife."

"Your wife?"

"Yeah. They weren't anything dirty or nothin', but kinda sexy, you know. They weren't for anybody else to see. She didn't really want me to shoot 'em, but I promised her they were only for me. I stuck 'em in that book, and then when I remembered 'em and went lookin' for 'em, she told me she sold the book at the garage sale."

Margaret stood, lightheaded. "What is your name, son?"

"Charles. Charlie."

"But Elaine, your wife, calls you C., doesn't she?"

The young man smiled. "She sure does! You found my pictures, didn't you?"

"I didn't know they were from the book, but yes, I found them. I want you to have them, and I want you to have your ten dollars back."

"That's not necessary, ma'am."

"Oh, yes it is," she said, digging out a ten and the wrinkled envelope of pictures. When Charles stood, she embraced him long and hard.

"Somethin' wrong?" he said.

"Give your wife a hug for me," she said, her voice thick. "Young love is so sweet."

When he was gone, Margaret hurried to the kitchen where she knelt to ferret out Clinton's tightly wrapped remaining mints from behind the waste basket under the sink.

Still on her knees, she put the remaining mints in her mouth and chewed, letting the stale sweetness fill her throat. *Clinton had just found those pictures and was bringing them to show me at the game!*

"God, forgive me!" she sobbed. "Clinton, my sweet love, forgive me!"

DITCHED

N ot even Pastor Ingle knew what to do about it. How does one confront a person about bizarre behavior? Reports of strange goings-on with Patsy Little had begun more than two months before. *Such a dainty name for such a large woman,* he thought, but that was the least of it.

The pastor's wife had first mentioned it to him. "Something's not right with Pat Little," she said one evening.

He harumphed and said that wasn't news to him, then felt guilty. "Just because she's never been involved that much doesn't mean I should judge her," he said.

Patsy was in her late thirties, never married, lived alone in an expensive apartment building, bought a new car every year and a half, and financed her lifestyle with a mid-management marketing position. Despite being larger than the average woman by fifty or sixty pounds, she dressed well and didn't skimp on her hair or face.

Pastor Ingle hardly knew her, except that she was a regular attender of First Church and always pleasant on her way out. He never saw her come in, he recalled. Whenever he saw her, she was leaving. She never involved herself in anything but Sunday school and church, and—according to Mrs. Ingle—those in charge of other ministries had quit asking her.

"She always has excuses," the pastor's wife explained.

"Valid?"

"Sure, but don't we all have valid reasons not to get involved?"

Nigel cocked his head. "I suppose. What's she up to now?"

"Laureen says Patsy invited her to lunch and then disappeared."

"Patsy stood her up?"

"No. They met at a restaurant, got acquainted, enjoyed a little lunch, Patsy excused herself, and never came back."

"What'd Laureen do?"

"She waited and waited, then told the waitress she wanted to pay for their meal so she could check on her friend in the rest room without seeming to duck out on the bill. The waitress said the other lady had already paid. Laureen hurried to the ladies' room, but she couldn't find Patsy. She went out to the parking lot, and Patsy's car was gone."

"Did Laureen call her?"

"Tried. All she got was the answering machine."

"Did she try her at work?"

"Several times. Patsy's secretary says she gave the messages to Patsy. The girl said Patsy was very busy. Laureen asked her if Patsy was OK. The girl said, 'Never better.'"

The pastor shook his head. "Strange. What do people think?"

"Laureen isn't the type to tell people. I think I'm the only one who knows."

Nigel Ingle dismissed the news, telling himself it had to have been a communication problem. Maybe Patsy had become ill or forgot an appointment or something came up and she hadn't been able to properly excuse herself. In church the next Sunday she seemed fine, but that afternoon Mrs. Ingle told Nigel that Patsy had avoided Laureen.

"Laureen made a beeline for her right after the service, but Patsy ducked away."

Nigel pursed his lips. Should he involve himself in this niggling mystery when he had so much else to do? He decided no.

Two weeks later, it happened again. Patsy Little had taken the initiative, told Marjorie Grom that she wanted to get to know her better, and set a date for coffee and shopping. While they were trying on outfits at the mall, Patsy disappeared.

Same story as before. Marjorie waited for Patsy outside a changing room and finally began calling for her. She searched the store, the mall, and the parking lot. Eventually, Marjorie phoned Patsy's office. She was in but not available. Patsy never called back.

"Is Marjorie telling people this story?" Nigel asked his wife.

"She talks a little more than Laureen, but I don't think it's widespread."

"Has Laureen heard?"

"I told her. It was just too coincidental."

Nigel sat forward on the couch and rested his chin in his hands. "What do you make of it, Jen?"

"I'm at a loss," his wife said, moving next to him. "You have to wonder if the woman is losing her mind."

Nigel was surprised. "It's strange, but that bad?"

"It's too strange, hon," she said. "Something's wrong."

Nigel talked it over with Roger Rhodes, his counseling pastor. "I don't know if it's encouraging or discouraging that you were unaware of it," he told Roger, smiling.

Roger nodded. "Either it's not a public issue yet, or I'm busier than I thought."

"What do you think, Rog? Should you talk to her?"

"Oh, it's a problem all right, but you know I never seek people out. That would make the counseling function—"

"I know," Nigel said, raising a hand, "that would make the counselors seem like policemen."

"People have to come to us with their problems. We're not disciplinarians. We're—"

"Counselors, I know," Nigel said. "Which makes me—"

"If not the disciplinarian, the guardian at the gate. Is this woman someone from whom you should protect your flock?"

"I hope not," the pastor said. "Is it wrong to hope for some sort of a chemical imbalance?"

Roger grinned. "You're truly a modern pastor."

"Seriously," Nigel said. "I'm praying the woman is all right, but she sure doesn't seem it."

Roger sobered. "Should we ask Sue?" he said, referring to someone on his staff. "She's a little more psychiatric than psychological, if you know what I mean."

They met with Sue Runnels the next morning. She was troubled by the story of Patsy Little. "I know this isn't news," she said, "but the woman is apparently pleading for help."

"By running?"

"It's almost like leaving a note," Sue said. "She's saying, 'I'm going to run from you, but don't ignore me. Please catch me.'"

"Catch her," the pastor repeated. "Is she doing something awful?"

Sue shook her head. "I'm only guessing, but abandoning lunch dates and shopping guests may be the worst of it. I hope so. But it's so blatant, such a breach of protocol for a woman of her station—"

"She knows better."

"Of course. She could never hold a job like she has if she ever ditched one client, even with a good reason."

"Is this just for attention then?"

Sue pressed her lips together. "I wish I knew her better. It's so hard to draw any conclusions. Sure, it's for attention, but not just attention. She wants to be confronted, to connect with someone. The question is why." Sue shook her head. "I haven't been of much help."

Roger asked Sue if there was a clue in Patsy's victims. "There might be," she said. "They are mirror images of one another, aren't they? Laureen and Marjorie, I mean. Mid-forties, upper middle class, children grown and gone or almost, husbands successful. Respected. Admired. Considered spiritual."

"Considered?" the pastor asked, wondering if Sue knew something he didn't about the women.

"Yes, people consider Laureen and Marjorie to be spiritually mature. I know I do."

He nodded. "What do we do?"

Sue thought for a moment. "We have to wait," she said. "With this having happened twice in fewer than three weeks, it's going to get around. Next time she asks someone out, it'll likely be someone who has heard these stories. Just hope she accepts and that we hear about it. We can watch and see what happens."

The pastor sat forward. "Sue, is it possible Patsy is confused sexually, is attracted to these women but panics when she gets close to making her feelings known?"

Sue raised her eyebrows. "It happens. But running away doesn't fit. If she lost her resolve, she would simply not make advances. This behavior seems designed to draw attention to herself. Let's not disappoint her."

"Should I call her in and confront her?" Nigel said.

"You might," Sue said, "but I could predict the response. She'd deny it, lie about it, or pretend to not hear you. She might change the subject. But if you wait and she ditches someone again, you'll really have her. She can't explain away three identical incidents."

More than a month later the news came to Pastor Ingle that Evelyn Pinder had been invited to lunch by Patsy Little. Evelyn, 50, was a choir member and primary Sunday school teacher. Her husband was an airline executive, and their three children were all college graduates.

"To tell you the truth, I've heard stories," the pleasant woman whispered to the pastor. "I'm scared. Is Patsy insane?"

Nigel asked Evelyn for her help. He summoned Roger and Sue, and they mapped out a strategy. Evelyn would accept the invitation and keep in touch with Sue. Sue would be in the vicinity at the time of the meeting and would keep an eye on Patsy.

The following Thursday Patsy was true to form. Evelyn admitted that she herself was nervous but that Patsy was cordial and conversational, asking Evelyn about her life and family.

"When she excused herself to go to the ladies room," Evelyn told the pastor later, "I knew she was gone."

Sue picked up the story. "I was in the mall, pretending to read a magazine. Patsy strode out of that restaurant as if it were the most natural thing in the world. I followed her to her car and greeted her.

"She says, 'Well, Miss Runnels, how nice to see you.' Just like that. I say, 'Didn't I see you with Evelyn Pinder?' She never misses a beat. 'Yeah, I ran into her, too. Small world.'

"I put my hand on her shoulder, and she stiffens. I say as earnestly and firmly as I can, 'Patsy, what's wrong?' She smiles and says, 'What do you mean?' I say, 'Evelyn told me she was meeting you here, so why did you tell me you just ran into her?'

"She says, 'It was just a figure of speech. OK, we met here for lunch.' I say, 'Patsy, where is Evelyn?' and she says, 'Probably on her way home, just like I'm on my way to work. See ya.'

"She wasn't smiling anymore and didn't look at me. I went straight back in to Evelyn."

Evelyn spoke up. "Patsy had already paid the check. Pastor, what is wrong with that girl?"

"I don't know," Nigel admitted, "but she probably needs more help than I can offer."

After Evelyn was excused, Sue said she had given more thought to the women who had been ditched. "They're nearly interchangeable," she said. "Patsy is punishing them, maybe getting back at her mother or some authority figure, some successful person."

"But she's successful," the pastor said. "Why should she resent success? I'm in over my head." Roger agreed that Patsy should be summoned to the pastor's office and that Sue should be there, if only as a witness.

The three agreed they had never seen Patsy with a man. "Meaning you should carry the conversation," Sue said. "She will likely see you as an authority figure and defer to you."

"That answers whether she will agree to see me without my telling her why."

"She will," Roger said.

Sue nodded. "She may even have an idea. It may be what she's wanted all along. I would be direct, if I were you. Not unkind. Tell her exactly what you know, and ask her straight out what it means. She may have never articulated it even to herself. Don't let her off the hook."

"You think she'll deny it?"

"She may, but I'm guessing she desperately wants you to cut through that. Without bullying her, insist on the truth. Keep her on track."

"This is more than a spiritual problem though, isn't it?" Nigel asked. "I had a few counseling courses, but if we're talking depression or something, I'm—"

Sue interrupted. "Call me overly spiritual, but I'm convinced that spiritual problems are at the root of mental problems. You get to the bottom of that, and you'll have a head start on the problem in the mind—pardon the pun."

"She'll need help beyond what I can give her."

"That's what Sue's here for," Roger said.

Pastor Ingle called Patsy at work. She sounded cheery. "I'd love to come by. What's up?"

"Just a matter I'd like to discuss."

"I'm not in trouble, am I?" she said, as if teasing.

"You can't get in trouble with me, Patsy."

"Sure I can. You're my pastor."

Patsy arrived pleasant and friendly, but Nigel saw her face cloud when Sue joined them. "I saw you earlier today, Miss Runnels," she said quietly.

The pastor explained Sue's presence. "By policy I don't meet with women alone. You know Sue, and if you don't mind, I'd like her to sit in with us."

"What if I did mind?" Patsy said.

Nigel stared at her. She had said it not unkindly, but seemingly out of curiosity.

"Then we would have someone of your choosing join us."

"Miss Runnels is fine," Patsy said.

Nigel and Sue shrugged and smiled. Sue arranged her chair so she was out of Patsy's peripheral vision. The pastor began.

"I want to talk about your inviting women to lunch and then abandoning them."

Patsy's face went blank, as if she had not heard him. She stared at his face, her lips parted as if to speak, but she said nothing.

Nigel saw Sue nod slightly, encouraging him. "Why do you do this?" he asked Patsy. "What are these women supposed to think? They worry about you, try to see you or call you, but you avoid them. Why?"

Patsy spoke softly. "I don't know too many people at this church. I thought it would be good if I got acquainted with some."

"Why did you choose Laureen, Marjorie, and Evelyn? They're all older than you, not one has a career, and each is married with mostly grown children."

Patsy shrugged. "I thought they would be interesting."

"And did you get to know them?"

"A little."

"Why did you leave them?"

"We had good conversations. I enjoyed our meetings."

"You're not answering me, Patsy. You know social manners. You travel and entertain in your job."

"Of course."

"Do you ever disappear from a business luncheon?"

"I thought it would be good to fellowship," she said. "I fellowshiped with them in the name of our Lord and Savior."

That last phrase startled the pastor. What was she trying to say, and why had she said it in such a quaint manner? "Do you think Jesus ever abandoned someone?" he asked.

"Our Lord never did anything wrong, Pastor."

"Have you done things wrong, Patsy?"

She shrugged. "Haven't we all?"

"I want you to answer a question for me, Patsy," Nigel said. "Will you do that?"

She nodded.

"I don't want you to pretend not to hear me or change the subject. OK?"

She nodded again.

"Why were you rude to those women?"

He looked carefully for signs of weakening. Her face was empty. But at least she had not changed the subject.

"Why?" he repeated.

She neither moved nor spoke.

"Is that something Jesus would do?" he asked.

She whispered, "Our Lord would not do that."

She was stalling, but she was not lying. He waited. He loved this tortured soul with as pure a pastoral love as he had in him. She was typical of the reason he had got into the pastorate. It was people like her, people who needed contact and personal ministry, who made him feel more of a shepherd when he returned from seminars and conventions.

His first two pastorates had been smaller works with no staff. He had been everything to his people. He knew how to delegate, but visiting, counseling, mediating had been all his. How long had it been since he had personally counseled someone deep in pain, someone so weighed down that even she didn't know why she did what she did?

As the late afternoon sun played through the blinds, Sue Runnels faded into the shadows. The beautiful desk and the deep-grained wood bookcases seemed to melt away. Nigel Ingle was a young man again, a personal minister, a man with a flock. He was not the man who carried pedigrees and honors, who was in demand throughout the state.

The woman across from him was not a career woman with a mental disease. She was a parishioner, a needy soul. He had nothing else on his mind, nothing else to do. He quit worrying about his qualifications or what to do with her. The trappings of the years and his own successes fell away. His heart, his spirit, his soul emerged. His mind was renewed with sensitivity to her and to God. Silently he pleaded for something, anything that would prove a balm for this poor woman.

Oh, that God would speak to him and through him in his weakness! He recalled from a decade past when he had counseled people and advised them with a wisdom far beyond his years because he got out of the way and let God speak. "Father," he prayed within, "what would You have me say to this woman?"

He didn't want to ask her why again. He knew she was asking that herself. That was why she was here. She did not want to be asked why. She wanted to be told why. She wanted relief, healing, forgiveness, restoration. If her actions appeared bizarre to others, how must they seem to her?

Pastor Ingle rose and moved around the front of his desk to a chair next to Patsy. She did not follow him with her eyes but stared at the chair behind his desk. He pulled next to her now and rested his hand on the arm of her chair.

He spoke barely above a whisper. "Patsy, did someone do something hurtful to you when you were a child, something you didn't like?"

She did not turn, but he saw her face contort and her eyes fill. When she spoke he squinted and leaned forward. "Fatsy Patsy," she mouthed. The words barely reached the air.

"I'm sorry?" he said.

"Patricia," she said, a tear breaking loose. "My name is Patricia, but they called me Fatsy Patsy."

"Who called you that?"

"Everyone."

He knew it wasn't true. Her family, at least her parents, could not have called her that. She must have had one friend, one sensitive teacher, someone.

"Patricia, did someone abandon you?"

She didn't respond.

"When you were little," he suggested. "Did someone leave you alone?"

She turned to stare at him and spoke in a monotone. "We were jumping rope," she said, "and everyone ran away. I tried to catch them, but they were skinny and strong and outran me. I thought it was a game. I ran and ran, but they got farther and farther from me. When I saw them again, they wouldn't tell me why. Nobody seemed to know what I was talking about. But it happened again and again." Patsy fought to keep her lips from trembling.

"Patricia, did you lose one of your parents when you were young?"

She turned away and whispered. "How did you know my mother died?"

"When?" he asked.

"When I was twelve."

Twelve! The number screamed at him. This devastated child, in the hormone-raged bloom of puberty, was abandoned not only by those she thought were friends, but also by her mother.

"And your father?"

"He sent me to my aunt."

Abandoned again.

"What happened there?"

"The convenience store happened there," she said flatly. "Our Lord didn't hear my prayers."

"Tell me."

"We were looking at magazines. They all ran out. Just like before. I was ditched."

"And you prayed?"

"All the time. I asked our Lord and Savior to make my friends like me, but He didn't hear me."

"Your aunt?"

"She told my dad he could have me back when I was out of high school. By then he was remarried, and they both drank. I put myself through college, moved here, got a job, tried to make something of myself."

Nigel was tempted to praise her, to tell her she had done a wonderful, magnificent thing. She had pulled herself up, become someone, showed them all. But she hadn't. She was as blind to her success as beautiful women often are to their beauty.

"But you think you failed again, don't you?" the pastor tried, knowing he was in a counselor's no-man's-land. He was tempted to peek at Sue Runnels to see if she was cringing.

"Yes," Patsy said. "I failed again. And our Lord still doesn't hear me."

"Jesus never fails," Nigel said, wondering himself why he had resorted to a cliché here, now. Patsy seemed to flinch at his reference to Jesus.

"Jesus Christ our Lord and Savior," she said, as if correcting him. What was it with her formal references, her insistence on "our" Lord and Savior?

"Is Jesus personal to you, Patricia?" he said. "Is Jesus Christ *your* Lord and Savior?"

"He's everyone's Lord and Savior," she said. "Some get Him to listen and some don't."

Nigel wanted to shout that it was a lie. Jesus was not everyone's Lord or Savior unless they received Him, and no one "gets Him" to listen. But she was fragile. The oozing wound of her life had been exposed.

"The ones who get Him to listen are the ones who are married and happy, right?" he said. "The ones whose lives are successful because they have loving, supportive husbands."

She nodded. "And they're just like those kids who called me names and ditched me," she said through clenched teeth.

"But you're showing them, aren't you?" Nigel said. "You're paying them back."

Patsy buried her face in her hands and wept. "I'm trying to," she sobbed.

"And are you paying Him back too?"

She said nothing.

"Are you paying Jesus back for abandoning you?"

She nodded. "Our Lord and Savior."

Nigel sat back and caught Sue's eye. She raised a fist of motivation to him. Now he began a slow, steady explanation of Jesus Christ to Patricia Little.

He told her God loved her. He told her Jesus had died for her sins, yes, hers personally. "If God does not hear your prayers, it's because you have not trusted Christ to forgive your sins and believed in Him."

It was a revelation. Her faith, her religion had been impersonal, institutional. She'd had some drive, mostly fueled by revenge. She had lived to prove herself, to pay back her tormentors—all those who had abandoned her, including, in her mind, "our Lord and Savior Jesus Christ."

Nigel led her to Christ that day. She finally understood. She smiled through her tears at the joy of it, but part of her still felt bad. She prayed for forgiveness for her bitterness and how it had manifested itself, but still she felt ugly about how she had treated the women of the church.

"They will forgive you," Nigel assured her. "They will be thrilled for you."

They agreed that she still needed counseling. "And I'd like to track down just one of those girls from that day in the convenience store," she said. "I want to know if even one remembers."

Sue had promised not to say anything, so now she raised her hand. Nigel smiled and nodded to her.

"That would be part of the counseling if you'd let us help you, Pats—Patricia," Sue said. "It would be important for you to reconnect with some of the painful memories."

The women of First Church rallied round Patricia Little, though the counseling was painful. A call to her father resulted in an angry exchange and a slamming down of the phone. But the news Pastor Ingle received of Patricia's finally tracking down an old nemesis confirmed his decision to keep his huge church personal at any cost.

Sue and Patricia finally traced one of the girls and found her married name listed in Cleveland. Patsy dialed and a woman answered. "Is this the Terri who used to live on Woods Street and grew up with Patsy Little?"

"Yes."

"Well," Patricia said with a sigh, "this is Patsy. My counselor is listening because I need to deal with a few old wounds."

"Oh, Patsy!" Terri said, "please tell me it's really you!"

"It's really me."

"You don't know how many times I've tried to get hold of you over the last year! I've never forgotten how awful we were to you. It's bothered me all my life. Can you ever forgive me?"

NIGHT STRANGER

Reggie Ingle nearly missed seeing the hitchhiker. A long stretch of Kellogg Road was unlit, and the thin young man appeared only briefly in Reggie's headlights. Yet when Reggie braked, he saw nothing behind him. He honked once and waited. Hearing and seeing nothing, he lifted his foot from the brake. As he was about to accelerate, the passenger door opened.

"Thanks, man," the guy said. "Nice wheels."

Reggie nodded. Before the door shut he noticed that the young man wore docksiders, no socks, tight blue jeans, a maroon college sweatshirt, and a baseball cap. "Where to?" Reggie said.

"Just to the highway. Lonely stretch here. Dark."

Reggie wheeled the Trans Am back out onto the road. When was the last time anyone told him he had a nice car? All he had heard about this car, for which he was in hock up to his ears, was that a pastor's son shouldn't drive something so— pick your own adjective: flashy, expensive, hot, showy. Though his father hadn't paid a dime of it, he allowed Reggie to live at home while taking some courses, so the pastor took as much heat for the "nice wheels" as Reggie did.

His father wasn't thrilled about the car either, but he was a fair man and admitted he was grateful he had no serious worries about his youngest son. They disagreed some on modes of worship, and Reggie was more comfortable with experience-oriented faith than his father was, but otherwise they got along well.

"I'm going west as far as First Church," Reggie told the stranger.

"That's OK. I'll just get out at the highway."

"I've got time to run you west a little further if you need me to."

"No, thanks."

Reggie cocked his head but kept his eyes on the road. Who ever heard of a hitchhiker who didn't want to get as close to his destination as possible? It seemed from his tone that conversation was not a priority. Reggie was wrong. Presently, the young man opened up.

"Look, you could do me a favor?"

"Depends."

"Do you know anybody in Forest Lake?"

It was the suburb to the west of Reggie's own. "A few, sure."

"You don't happen to know the MacKenzies."

Reggie pursed his lips. "Sorry. Don't think so."

"Blonde daughter named Barb, mid-twenties. Beautiful."

"My loss. Nope. Friend of yours?"

"We used to go together."

"You want me to take you there? It's not far."

"No, no. It's just that I've got some stuff of hers from when we dated. I know she'd want it back, but I'd rather not see her. Know what I mean?"

Reggie nodded. "It happens. You'd rather not deal with the pain."

"Exactly."

"Broke your heart, did she?"

"Well, actually I broke hers. I went off to Albion College and sort of never came back."

"Found somebody new?"

"Not really. Well, sort of."

"You want me to drop something off to her?"

"It's too much to ask."

"Just tell me where she lives."

"I don't know. A stranger showing up, giving her stuff from me. Not one of my better ideas."

"I'll just tell her straight out. I picked you up, and you asked me to do this."

"You'd do it, really?"

"The way you described her, I'd be crazy not to."

Reggie thought that was funny, but the young man didn't laugh. He dug into the pocket of his tight jeans, and his Detroit Tiger cap brushed the low ceiling. "Right up here will be fine," he said, nodding toward the highway frontage road.

"Are you sure? I'd be glad to take you."

"No, if you could do this for me, I'd really appreciate it."

He produced from his pocket a tiny class ring, a sorority pin, and a heavily creased wallet photo of a pretty blonde. "High school," he said, holding it under the light.

Reggie turned it over. "You mind?" he asked before reading.

The young man shook his head.

"To Edward with all my love forever. Barb."

"Edward, huh?"

"That's me."

Reggie noticed that though Edward had thick, dark eyebrows, the hair showing under his cap was buzzed almost to the skin.

"I should be doing this myself, man," Edward said. "If it's too much to ask, just say so, because—"

"Hey, I don't mind. You don't mind if I tell her I picked you up?"

"You don't have to say where, do you? You don't know where I'm going."

"You don't want her to find you? You haven't changed your mind about her?"

Edward shook his head. "I'd mail the stuff, but then there'd be a postmark. I don't know. You don't have to if you don't want to."

Reggie insisted and took the directions from Edward. Something in him enjoyed this. He had no knowledge, no responsibility, just a delivery to make.

"See you around," he told Edward as he left the car.

"No, you won't," Edward said softly. "But I sure appreciate this."

As Reggie pulled onto the ramp for the highway he saw Edward in his rearview mirror, hands jammed into his pockets, shoulders hunched against the evening chill. Then he seemed to disappear in the darkness. Reggie glanced at his watch. Nearly nine-thirty. Not too late for a social call. Forest Lake was ten minutes away.

The house at the address Edward had given him was lit and active. Guests were leaving. Reggie parked in the street so as not to block their car. He felt awkward approaching the door when the people were exchanging hugs and kisses and good-byes.

"Night, Mom. Night, Dad."

"Night, honey. Bye, Steve."

The foursome turned as one to stare at Reggie. "May I help you?" the older man said.

"Gotta go," the young woman said, arm in arm with the one they'd called Steve.

"I'm looking for Barb," Reggie said. "Barb MacKenzie."

The young woman stopped and spun around. "I'm Barb," she said.

"Oh, your hat must have covered your blonde hair."

Reggie had said it pleasantly enough, but no one smiled.

"Do I know you?" she said, squinting in the dim light, clearly trying to recognize him.

He shook his head but didn't know what to say now that he had found her with another boyfriend. "I, uh, have something for you from an old friend."

"What?"

"Well, maybe we should speak privately."

She said nothing, and her companion looked to her father. "I don't want to be rude," the older man said, "but surely you don't expect her to speak privately with you before she even knows who—"

"I'm sorry," Reggie said quickly. "I don't mean to be so mysterious. I just happened to pick up a hitchhiker who asked if I'd do him a favor and bring some stuff back to you for him."

"Who?" Barb said. "What?"

Reggie hesitated, his hands in his jacket pockets, looking first to Barb and then at her escort. "It's OK," she said.

With a larger audience than he had expected, Reggie pulled the trinkets from his pocket and pressed them into her hand. He didn't want to be guilty of making them obvious if she chose to keep them hidden. But she held them up to the porch light and did a double take, staring at them as if trying to remember something or make it all make sense. Reggie had a fleeting thought that poor Edward might be glad he wasn't seeing this. The woman appeared not to remember to whom she had given her ring and pin and picture.

But when she spoke, her voice was thick. "Where did you get these?" she managed.

"Edward," Reggie said.

Her knees buckled, and Steve caught her.

"Take her inside," her father said.

Reggie stepped aside as three-fourths of the party disappeared. The father stepped out onto the cement steps in his stocking feet. "Where did you get that stuff?" he demanded.

"I told you, sir. I picked up a hitchhiker. Edward. He asked if I would bring this stuff back to his old girlfriend. That's all I know. I'm sorry."

"What did this Edward look like?"

"Tall, short hair, dark eyebrows, skinny."

"What was he wearing?"

"Jeans, an Albion sweatshirt. Tiger cap."

The man moved past Reggie and leaned over, his hands on the wrought iron railing. He stared at the ground. "What did he say?"

"Just what I said."

"Nothing else?"

"Just that he used to date Barb until he went off to college. Then they drifted apart."

The man lifted his head and sighed. He turned to face Reggie. "If this is some kind of a prank, it's not funny. If it's not, I'd like you to come in and answer a few questions."

Reggie looked at his watch. He wasn't sure he wanted to get into this.

"Oh, so it is a prank," the man said, "and you're gonna just race off to tell your friends what kind of a reaction you got."

"No, sir. I'm from the next town. My dad is pastor at First Suburban. I'm telling you straight just what happened. This guy asked me to—"

"Save it for the others."

As Mr. and Mrs. MacKenzie sat holding hands and Steve sat with his arm around Barb, she wept openly as Reggie recounted the story, every detail. He was startled to notice that Steve and Barb wore matching wedding bands.

"I'm Barb Fisher now," she said.

"So, how long has it been since you've heard from Edward?"

Barb hid her face in her hands. "Tell him, Daddy."

"Mr., ah—"

"Ingle. Reggie."

"Reggie, our daughter was engaged to marry Edward Dodge. She was even willing to marry him after he contracted leukemia two and a half years ago and lost all his hair. His outlook appeared bleak, and a bone marrow transplant failed."

"No wonder he looked so thin," Reggie said.

"Reggie," Mr. MacKenzie said carefully, "Edward has been dead nearly two years. We attended his funeral."

Reggie stood quickly. "Well, people, I'm sorry. Someone is pulling an awful prank on you and put me right in the middle of it. Believe me, I never saw this guy before in my life. I had no reason not to believe him. Please, forgive me. I had no idea."

"Sit down, son," Mr. MacKenzie said. "I want you to help us find this person. I'd like to make him regret this. Barb met Steve and was putting her grief behind her—with his help. Now this. Can you be as specific as possible and tell us again what he looked like?"

Before Reggie could speak, Barb jumped to her feet, crying. "Daddy, don't you see? It *was* Edward! I knew he would try to communicate with me! I just knew it! It was him!"

"His ghost?" her mother said, her voice barely above a whisper. "You think Edward's spirit is trying to contact you?"

"Nonsense!" her father said.

"Oh, I don't think so either," Reggie said, suddenly wanting to be anywhere but there. How had he got himself into this? "It's a sick joke," he added. "Someone's idea of a—"

"No!" Barb wailed. "No! Steve, you agree with me, don't you?"

Steve looked stricken. Clearly he believed his wife had gone over the brink. He looked pleadingly to her parents.

"Tell me!" Barb demanded. "You agree, don't you?"

"Barb, I never knew Edward. I don't know any of his friends. I can't imagine anyone doing this to you."

"It isn't anyone, Steve! It's Edward! He's telling me it's OK that I married you! The last of my personal stuff is back, the stuff I would have wanted to give only to my husband." She held it out to Steve, but he recoiled.

"You don't want it?" Barb said, nearly hysterical. "Edward has given it back to me for you, don't you see?" Steve reached for it, but she jerked it away. "You don't see! You don't agree! You're jealous of Edward!"

"Well, why shouldn't he be, honey?" her father said. "You're not making sense!"

"Daddy!"

With that she marched upstairs. Steve followed her but soon returned. "She's convinced that the guy you picked up tonight was Edward's ghost," he said, dropping to the couch.

"Unbelievable," Mr. MacKenzie spat. "A grown woman."

"Well," his wife said, seeming to straighten her back for courage. "That makes two grown women."

"You believe this nonsense?" her husband said.

"Just don't rule it out because you don't understand it," she said. She joined her daughter upstairs.

"This guy didn't do anything ghost-like, did he?" Mr. MacKenzie said. "He didn't levitate or disappear or anything?"

Reggie smiled and shook his head, not wanting to admit that twice it seemed that Edward had disappeared. "He wasn't dressed for the weather, and he wasn't carrying any luggage. That was kind of strange. And he must have been walking a long time unless he somehow talked someone into letting him off near the woods at the unlit portion of Kellogg Road."

"You picked him up on Kellogg?"

"On my way back from school."

"How far in?"

"A couple of miles."

"Who would walk that far in this weather?"

Steve sat up. "I don't know whether I'm jealous of a dead man or if I think there could be anything to this."

"Could I see a picture of Edward?" Reggie said.

Mr. MacKenzie got one from the other room. Reggie stared at it in silent disbelief.

"Your dad being a pastor, I don't suppose you go for this kind of thing, eh, Ingle?" Mr. MacKenzie said.

"Not until now," he said, the eight-by-ten in his hands. "This is the guy I picked up tonight."

Reggie Ingle had long felt his father was too closed to supernatural manifestations of God, so he was pleasantly surprised now to sit across from him in the family room and note his lack of snap judgment. Nigel Ingle was hearing his son out.

"That's a fascinating story," he said at last, setting down his tea cup and smoothing his robe around him. "What do you make of it?"

"I can't rule out that this guy appeared in the road and disappeared later," Reggie said. "Now, Dad, don't look at me that way. You've been with me all along."

"You hadn't declared yourself till now, Reg. What do you do with the fact that the Bible says it's appointed unto a man once to die and after that the judgment?"

"I believe the Bible, Dad. But why couldn't his spirit come back and comfort his grieving former love?"

"Do you also believe that God is a God of order, One who never changes and never fails?"

"Of course."

"Then wouldn't God have a better idea? Wouldn't He have better timing?"

"I don't follow."

"You said yourself that the girl had put the tragedy behind her and was getting on with her life. Was this comforting to her to have the ghost of her dead fiancé return and put tension in her marriage? Why couldn't Edward have come back sooner? Too much paperwork in heaven's travel agency?"

"You'd scold me for that kind of sarcasm."

"Sorry, but let's use our heads. If this was divine, it would have some of the divine in it. Wouldn't Edward have a message of hope, of healing, of salvation? Would he not speak some word from God?"

Reggie didn't respond. His father was awfully hard to argue with. "Dad," he said finally, "what do you make of it?"

"You've had it right all along, Reggie. It's a sick joke."

"So you think some friend of Edward's made himself look like Edward, stopped the first car heading the right direction, and lured an unsuspecting fool into his prank."

Pastor Ingle nodded. "Except for the friend part. This was not a friend of Edward's."

"How could you know that?"

"This was someone who knew such a visit would upset this Barb. It was not funny. It was perpetrated by an enemy. Hers or her late fiance's."

"Sick. You're making a lot of sense, Dad, but I've got to tell you, it's more fun to think this might all be true."

"That it was Edward's ghost."

"Yeah."

"Leave that to the entertainers, Reg."

"Well, let's say you're right. In my gut I find it hard to believe, but if it was a bad joke, I have to do something about it. I was used. It hurt to see that girl so upset, and her poor husband!"

Reggie's father rose and took their cups to the kitchen. "I like your thinking, Reggie. Focus on the people and their pain rather than on fantasy. That'll help you find out what's going on. You're not going to be satisfied until you do, anyway, so you might as well carve out some time to investigate. You always wanted to be a cop."

"Yeah. Till I grew up."

"And now you don't know what you want to be. So be a cop."

Reggie started at the community college he attended. He figured a prankster wouldn't take the chance of being picked up by someone he knew, so he hitchhiked on a lonely road that led from the campus to the other suburbs, but at night. If he was a student, he probably attended during the day. Reggie hung around the campus social center in the mornings before going to work in the afternoons. His patience wore thin near the end of two weeks. He saw no one who matched the description of Edward, and he didn't know how to begin to ask around.

He kept in touch with Mr. MacKenzie, who reported that his daughter was separated from her husband. "It's a shame," the man said, swearing. "This was a good marriage, and Steve is a nice boy. Barbara had been good about not pining away for Edward. No husband wants to compete with someone from the past, even if he's dead. But this business—this has Barb so upset that she can think or talk of nothing else. Steve felt he had to move out."

"Was that what she wanted?"

"I'm sure not, but she pushed him away."

"I'm sorry."

"It's not your fault. You got used."

Did I ever, Reggie thought. That was enough to make him stay at the task. His persistence paid off during the next week. As on the night he picked up the hitchhiker, he almost missed him.

Reggie's technique had been to pretend to read, all the while searching every male face and frame, looking for the short-haired, lanky collegian who had duped him. The problem was that the books and magazines he brought drew him into a story or chapter.

That was the problem when he nearly missed "Edward" the second time. The guy was not wearing the same outfit he had worn that night. The cap bore the Cincinnati C, and the sweatshirt was from Colorado. He wore white socks, but the shoes and the jeans were the same. The other stuff was close enough to what he had worn, and his hair had grown appropriately in the meantime.

Reggie had been reading, not watching, but he recognized the voice. Edward was bantering with a red-headed coed, but she didn't call him Edward. She called him Gary. Reggie stared at Gary's back and hid behind the magazine as he turned around. The eyebrows were lighter but just as bushy. And that face. It was him.

Reggie fought the urge to accost Edward/Gary. The man slipped on a jacket, then pulled the girl to him for a quick kiss. Reggie followed him to the parking lot and saw him get into a beat-up sedan. Keeping his distance, he trailed him for more than thirty miles to an apartment complex. Reggie parked at one corner of the lot and saw the ghost hitchhiker enter a glassed-in foyer and push a button.

Half an hour later the young man emerged and headed for his car. *Now what?* Reggie wondered. *Do I follow him or try to figure out who he came to see? How will I know? I don't even know Edward's or Gary's last name.*

He walked to the foyer and scanned the name on dozens of mailboxes. His breath caught when he saw "S. Fisher."

He tried to tell himself it was a common name, that he had nothing to go on. Anyway, what would he say if it *was* Barb's husband? He rang the buzzer.

"Yes?"

Reggie lowered his voice. "Me again. Forgot somethin'."

The door buzzed and Reggie hurried through to the elevator, knowing he had struck pay dirt but wondering what he was going to do now. He knocked at apartment 1210, and when Steve Fisher opened the door, Reggie stuck his foot in. "Couple of questions," he said, as Steve tried to keep him out.

"I have nothing to say to you," Steve said.

"Oh, then I'll just tell your wife and your in-laws that I ran into Edward's ghost at school and followed him to your place."

"I don't know what you're talking about."

"Quite a coincidence, I think," Reggie said. "They'll think so too."

"I don't care what they think."

Reggie shook his head. "You don't even deny it. If you were trying to get out of a marriage, why didn't you just say so?"

"It isn't that easy. I didn't always want out. I hoped she would forget her sainted dead boyfriend."

"This was sure a stupid way."

"Oh, I gave up on that long ago. This was just to push her to where she'd be impossible to live with."

"How did you do it?"

"It was easy. I found that stuff among her junk when we moved. Edward's folks must have given it to her after the funeral, and she either never went through it or forgot about it."

"So you found someone who looked like Edward and—"

Steve nodded. "I got so tired of hearing about this perfect person, I thought I was gonna explode. Every day, something else about Edward. And at her parents' place I was complimented every time about how good I was about letting her have her memories. When I couldn't stand it anymore, I dug through her stuff for a picture of him. She had plenty. I guess one of his favorite outfits in the hospital was that Albion sweatshirt and that Tiger cap. Those were easy enough to get. My friend darkened his eyebrows and looked just like Edward right before he died."

"He sure did."

Steve looked at his watch. "So, I s'pose you're gonna blow the whistle on me."

"You bet I am. You're a rotten guy."

"I'm gonna deny everything."

"Do whatever you want. Maybe they won't believe me."

"They won't."

"I've got to ask you: why did you make it so complicated? Why didn't you just tell Barb and her parents that they were driving you crazy with Edward? Don't you think if they knew they would have tried to get her some help? I mean, you married her too soon. She needed more time."

Steve looked at his watch again. "I've got a lot to do today."

"Just tell me why, and I'm out of here."

Steve sighed. "Let's just say Edward wasn't the only thing wrong with our marriage."

Reggie heard keys jangling and one in the door. Had Steve silently signaled someone? Steve looked as stricken as Reggie felt.

When the door opened the other thing wrong with Steve and Barb Fisher's marriage came into the apartment. "Oh, sorry, sweetie," the red-headed coed said. "I didn't know you had company."

She sat on the arm of Steve's chair. He pretended not to notice. "He was just leaving," Steve said.

Reggie rose, smiling broadly. With his hand on the door he said, "Well, you can probably expect a call from your father-in-law soon," he said. "You know what's most interesting about this?"

Steve didn't answer. He sat with his head in his hands while the red-head stared at Reggie.

"What's most interesting is that at school, Red here and Gary are an item. Guess you'd call that a double, double, double cross."

As Reggie left he saw Steve look sharply at his girlfriend. She moved away from him, protesting. Reggie wondered what kind of a scheme Steve would devise to free himself of her.

Early that evening, Reggie wheeled into the MacKenzie driveway. He asked to meet the three of them together. "I have a story to tell you," he began. "One you're not going to like, but which you'll be glad you heard." He didn't enjoy breaking bad news, but he couldn't wait to tell his own father.

A MIDNIGHT CLEAR

Lefty Boyle wrapped a Colt .44 magnum in an oily cloth and stuffed it under the front seat of his eleven-year-old Dodge. The station wagon, like Lefty, was running on empty.

He had traded four cans of gray, basement floor primer for the gun. Not a bad deal, he decided, since he had appropriated —as he liked to put it—the paint from his last employer. He had been out of work for six weeks.

Lefty hated guns. They were heavy, explosive, violent, uncontrollable things, not unlike himself. A friend once let him shoot his .38. One shot had been enough. Loud and awful. The .44 was even bigger, more powerful. Legend said the victim would never hear the shot, especially if the victim himself had pulled the trigger.

That was Lefty's plan.

He was a loser. He knew it. His three ex-wives, his four kids (two by women he had never married), his late father, and his aging mother knew it all too well. Everything he had ever touched had turned to dust. He was forty years old with nothing to live for.

Merry Christmas.

Late on December 24, seventy-year-old Evangeline sat before the front window of her tiny, ramshackle house. On her lap was a guide to prescription drugs. She had the ingredients. She just didn't want them to taste bad or cause pain. What she wanted was a sleepy death that would look like an accident. For though she hoped her death would hurt the family that had hurt her so, she didn't want them embarrassed. The last thing she wanted was to be a burden.

That meant she would have to burn the guide. If that were found, people might know. They must not know.

Evangeline was not one to beg. Sure, she wanted to see her children, especially on holidays. If they were too busy, that was all right. But how about a card, a call, something? How was it possible that her October birthday passed unnoticed? At Thanksgiving, not a word. And now Christmas.

God bless that big church! She had received her only birthday mail from the Women's Missionary Society at First Suburban. Tonight the junior high youth group had serenaded her with carols. They thought her tears were from joy, because she had managed to smile as she wept.

She begged their forgiveness for not having hot chocolate or Christmas cookies, lying that her kids and grandkids had just left, and there were no leftovers. The sponsor, puzzled, apologized for having thought she was a shut-in. "We had it down that you haven't been to church for several weeks. But you look good."

"Been traveling," she said, lying again. "My kids are pretty spread out, you know."

But they didn't know. They didn't know she despaired of her life. They were nice, but they hardly knew her name. And all their kindnesses made her family look only worse. Much as she tried to make excuses for her own kin, they had proved to her that she was worthless.

Lefty was merely cruising. He drove past a factory at which he had once worked. He snorted. Some deal. Only place he ever got promoted. Celebrated by getting drunk, coming in late the next day, getting reprimanded and put on probation, then fired for arguing about it with his boss. Well, maybe a little more than arguing. That cost him his second wife.

It also sent him back to Alcoholics Anonymous. They always loved to see him coming; he was a classic. He could stay sober for months, but when he disappeared he might not turn up again for a year. Christmas Eve might be a fun night to surprise 'em. There was always a crowd on holidays, and he would get the typical sympathetic welcome. Nah. He didn't need that.

What he needed, he was sure, was a bullet to the brain. Sweet peace. Sweet relief. Unending sleep. He chuckled at the irony of the few singles in his pocket. To keep driving he would have to spend a couple of them for gas. Every time he did that he lessened the amount of booze he could afford to medicate himself in advance of the big moment. The alcohol would camouflage fear, break down natural resistance, dull survival instinct. He talked himself out of taking a tall tale to A.A. before heading out for his pint and his private going-away party.

At a stoplight he emptied his pockets and discovered he couldn't afford both gas and good booze. He drove to the only station he knew that didn't require paying first after dark, pumped himself four gallons, and drove off. He wasn't even noticed. The story of his life.

Evangeline had never liked her name. She was the eldest of seven born to a farmer who had ignored—to his everlasting regret—a call to the ministry. He had preached a little, done some local missionary work, and been an active layman most of his life. But he had disobeyed, he told his children—Evangeline, Matthew, Mark, Luke, Chastity, Ruth, and Cletus—and that's why his crops were seldom blessed.

Poor Clete, Evangeline thought. The only kid born late enough to escape Daddy's trying to make up to God by naming his kids like saints, and he winds up with a moniker like that. How many times had that poor child heard, "I woulda thought they'da named you John!"?

Evangeline had been devout for a period in her teens. Something clicked for her at the little country church, and she had cried tears of true repentance and dedication. God became personal. Jesus was a Friend she could talk to and live for. How long ago had that been? What had happened?

Her daddy had been caught with the wife of his hired man, and though he denied everything till the day he died, Evangeline knew the truth. She could see it in her mama's eyes. Maybe that's what made Evangeline run off with the first man who said he loved her.

It had been a mistake from the beginning. She knew almost immediately, but divorce was not an option in those days. Not like now. She liked to say she had stopped counting the divorces her six kids had between them. But she hadn't stopped. She knew. Fourteen. Only one son was still with his first wife.

Evangeline had babies and raised kids in poverty with a man who ignored her and with whom she fell out of love. She didn't complain. She had made her choice, and she had a job to do. Unfortunately, her job consisted of thousands of unending tasks. She did everything for everybody in the house, from making scant rations go around to sewing and washing everyone's clothes, to cleaning up after everyone.

Why did she do it? Other women in her situation let their places go. She couldn't do that. Though her kids took her for granted and even criticized her, the work gave her life structure, a framework, a reason. She kept doing it until the children drifted away and her husband died.

She could get the kids to go to church with her only until they were about twelve. Then each followed the others' example and dropped out. "Dad never goes! Billy Ray got to quit when he was a teenager!"

Now, when weather permitted, she went to First Suburban alone. But it was a six-block walk to the bus. She went to the Women's Missionary Society once and got on their roll. That resulted in the occasional card or a we-missed-you note. How she longed for a message like that from even one of her kids. But they were busy, had their own lives.

It began to snow and accumulated quickly. Lefty heard the crunching under his tires whenever he drifted to the shoulder. He wanted to see the town from his favorite perch at lovers' lane on this his last night on earth. No one would be there on Christmas Eve, would they?

Wrong. Several had the same idea. He pulled into a spot in a long line of cars with fogged windows. Was it because it was Christmas that the lights below made him think of Bethlehem? He heard the famous song every year, but when was the last time he had thought about Bethlehem?

There had been a stretch when he took his two older boys to Sunday school and church. He even went himself a few times. When he was a kid he prayed a prayer with a teacher and she told him he'd been saved. He didn't understand it then and didn't want to think about it now. Far as he could remember, he'd never had a prayer answered. Not one. Either the whole deal was a sham, or he had missed some crucial detail.

There was no lessening of Lefty's resolve as he sat there watching the snow build on the hood of his Dodge. His was a drafty old rig, and every time he restarted the engine to clear the window and get a little heat on the floor, the thing knocked and rattled.

A cop came by and tapped on the windows of various cars, reminding occupants that they were welcome but that "there are still laws against certain things in this town." Seeing only one head above the seat in Lefty's car, the cop shined his flashlight throughout the car.

"You alone, pal?"

Lefty nodded and smiled sheepishly.

"This how you get your kicks?" the cop said. "You some kinda pervert?"

Lefty's smile vanished. He thought of storming out of the car. He thought of asking if peeking into parked cars was how the cop got *his* kicks. He even thought of pulling the .44 from beneath the seat and taking the cop with him in a blaze of glory.

But as usual, he acquiesced. "I'll move along if you want."

"That's what I want."

A nobody trying to be a somebody, Lefty thought as he started his car. But he didn't say it. He said things like that only when he was lubricated. Then he could claim it had been the booze talking. And he would be right. He never had to own up to anything.

He didn't want to go to a bar, and he was sure the package liquor stores would close by midnight. Lefty decided to buy his pint before making one last pass of his childhood home. What a dump that was! Few fond memories there.

Evangeline was startled to find herself hungry on this night of despair. Who would have thought the body would still crave nourishment when the mind knew the end was near? She wandered to the kitchen and looked in the refrigerator, carefully stepping over a puddle. The thing should have died years ago.

Inside she found a lone pickle spear in a jar of juice. No telling how old that might be. There was a half empty can of cat food for a kitty that had not come back from a date with Tom two weeks before. And there was a leftover piece of chicken. It did not appeal.

Evangeline sopped the floor with a dish towel and put a small pan of water on the stove. She rummaged for an ancient jar of bouillon cubes that had to be stale, despite their individual wrappings. When the water was near boiling, she crumbled a cube into a cup. Indeed stale. But all she wanted was the salty beef taste. Fresh or not, it would taste the same. How like her own history.

And how ironic this last supper. When she allowed herself to dream of her childhood, her happy memories revolved around the great dining room table. No one ate like farm men, and on Sundays, no one ate like a farmer's family. Two kinds of meat, lots of potatoes, steaming vegetables, ridiculously heavy and rich desserts.

She had tucked away a particularly precious mind picture of her mother smiling adoringly at her father, pre-trouble, as he told a guest missionary that he had not lost sight of his call and that he might yet one day follow God to the ends of the earth.

That day they were one big, happy, well-fed family. Her own had never been. Well-fed, maybe, but never harmonious. Alcohol had done that. Lack of interest in church had done that.

Lack of father-image had done that. But then she had grown up with a positive father model—at least for a time—and look how she turned out.

"Merry Christmas," the clerk said, bagging Lefty's pint. "Hope you've got somebody to share this with tonight."

"You want a pull?" Lefty said. He was sincere, beginning to take it from the sack.

"No, no. I don't even drink," the man said. "Just makin' conversation. Hate to see a man drink alone, 'specially on Christmas Eve."

If he only knew what else I was doing alone tonight! Lefty thought. This was one time he wouldn't care if he didn't finish the bottle. Used to be he prided himself on finishing before he passed out. No risk of spillage or theft that way. No waste. Tonight, or maybe during the first few minutes after midnight, he would waste himself. If there was a swallow or two left in the bottle, who would care? If he knew the answer to that, he wouldn't have had a .44 under the seat.

What am I waiting for? Evangeline asked herself as she sat by the window again. There was enough sodium Pentothal and phenobarbital in her various prescriptions to kill a twelve hundred-pound thoroughbred inside thirty seconds. She could have mixed it into her bouillon and enjoyed a sampling of at least the taste of the wonderful roasts her mother used to prepare. And then she would be gone. Painlessly. The crystalline power was odorless, so it would likely be tasteless.

It would be frightening and quick, but she could do it. She had decided that having no reason to live was reason enough to die. She sipped delicately at the hot bouillon, and the memories flooded back. Was it too much to expect that Jesus would accept her on Christmas Eve, even if she chose this most heinous way of getting there? Would she get there? She didn't know. It would be nice, but the point of this trip was not where she was going. It was what she was leaving.

Despite the ravages alcohol had brought Lefty Boyle, he couldn't deny the thrill of unsacking a fresh bottle, of breaking the seal by unscrewing the cap, of smelling the essence—once in a great while—of the really good stuff. And this was. Were it not for the fact that he wouldn't be here tomorrow, this was the kind of stuff that started, not ended, a binge. This was the stuff that would be your friend and lover and promise you anything.

Having been on the wagon since the day he had last worked, his throat was primed. Later he would savor the moment, play it out, open this bottle like a gift. Good stuff deserved ceremony, for it was a facilitator on the trip to oblivion.

Lefty packed the sack under his seat and heard it clink against the weapon. Now *there* was a combination of goodies. One quick and the other deadly. He would drive past his childhood home, return to lovers' lane, suck down the pint before the cop came back, and do the deed. *That,* officer, if you must know, is how I get my kicks. He smiled at the thought that this night would become legendary in the policeman's memories.

The bouillon was gone. Evangeline was weary. She sat, her cup on the small table before the window, with her hands in her lap, her head down, her shoulders slumped. Her lie to the singers nagged her. Did she need to confess it to have any chance of going to heaven? She didn't know. She simply wanted to get it over with and find out.

The old woman took her cup to the kitchen, turned the heat on under the water again, and rinsed out her cup. She unwrapped another square of bouillon and set it next to the cup. While the water heated, she moved to the bathroom where she studied her prescriptions. She transferred half a dozen capsules from each of two and put them in a third bottle. She didn't know how heat would affect them. She would not mix them in until her new drink began to cool.

While she stood in the kitchen, waiting, she heard one of the very few cars that went by her home that night. No Christmas parties in this neighborhood.

No Christmas tree at his mother's home, Lefty noticed. Well, he hoped nobody expected him to provide one. He didn't have one either. He guessed his mother liked Christmas though. Too bad. Looked like she was in bed. There was a light on in the tiny living room, but no one there. The light from the kitchen looked dim, as if it was the one over the stove. She always left that on. The rest of the place was dark, including the outside lights.

Where did the other people on this street get the money for decorations? They were as poor as Lefty's mother. Probably credit cards. Same things that nearly ruined him. He should have used one for a spree that night, he thought. By the time they caught him, he'd be farther gone than they could imagine.

He was excited about his plan but bone weary nonetheless. There was something about doing nothing, not working, having nowhere to go that left a man logy and listless. It would be so good to be rid of that feeling.

Lefty went around the block, wanting one last look at the old place with its leaning, one-car garage and the tiny backyard with the broken swing. When he came around again he pulled to the shoulder across the street and stared. What would be wrong with cracking open the pint for a preliminary sniff? He reached beneath the seat, hoping no one would see him and call the cops. Suspicious car on Dead End Street.

She waited until the water and the bouillon were tepid before stirring in the lethal dose. For some reason Evangeline felt a need to tidy the kitchen. She put away the bouillon jar, the pan, even the now empty prescription bottle. An autopsy would show what she had ingested, but without a note or any sign of distress, her demise would be ruled an accident. She could do at least that much for her children.

She carried her lukewarm cup of death to the living room, set it daintily on a mismatched saucer, and sat again. She had turned up the thermostat earlier and now buttoned her sweater, but she wondered if that would make her body decompose too quickly. She didn't want that. She wanted to appear to be sleeping in her chair by the window, and when no one could rouse her with the phone or doorbell, they would just take her away. No trouble. Not much bother. Nothing distasteful.

There was a car on the shoulder across the street, one that hadn't been there when she had gone to the kitchen. Looked like Luschel's old crate, or Lefty's, as he insisted on being called.

With the cap off, the essence of the whiskey hit Lefty's nostrils. It was all he could do to keep from inhaling the liquid as well. Strange, the stuff that had nearly killed him before he could do it himself smelled almost worth living for. But he would not. It would provide a farewell hit before the farewell shot.

He replaced the cap and the bottle and the sack and glanced up with a start to see his mother in her chair by the window. She couldn't see him, he knew, so he looked hard and long at her as he hadn't done for years. What had so effectively removed her from the forefront of his mind? When he left home twenty years before, he seemed to think of her every day. Even called her frequently. How long had it been? Would she feel betrayed if he left this life without even a good-bye? He couldn't tell her that's what it was, but of course he owed her at least that.

When the car door opened, the figure getting out sure looked like Luschel. Older, heavier, slower than Evangeline remembered, but as he gingerly made his way across the street, she knew it was him. Had he had some premonition about her? Would he be able to tell somehow that her death drink was on the table? This would have been easier if she had not had to face a living, breathing reminder of why she was doing it.

On the other hand, he had come. He had apparently thought about it, made a decision, driven over, and he was here. His visit didn't change her mind, but it was something. She fought the urge to make a litany of complaints. Where have you been? Why haven't you called? Why do I hear all my news about you from others? Don't you love me anymore? Did you forget my birthday? Why no call at Thanksgiving?

For some delicious reason she waited until she heard his knock before rising. The outside lights were off, so she could pretend to not have seen him approach. She even peered out through the crack with the door chain locked, as if to be sure of who it was.

"It's me, Mom."

"Luschel!"

"Lefty, Mom."

"Honestly, Luschel, you're not even left-handed."

"I know, but I always had to use that wrong-handed ball glove because we couldn't afford—"

"Let's not fight," she said, leading him to a chair next to hers. "Throw your coat anywhere."

"I'll leave it on. Just came to say Merry Christmas."

Suddenly Evangeline could not speak. He had come to wish her a good holiday? Was this sentiment she felt, or anger? The latter, surely, because the list of accusations was on the tip of her tongue. She imagined herself screaming, "I'm killing myself tonight, *tonight,* because of you!" And he would say, "Me, Ma? What'd I do?" And she'd tell him it was what he hadn't done, and he'd say, "What about the others?"

Well, the others were just as guilty, but he was here. He was the embodiment of the ills of the family. For some reason it had all fallen apart. They had drifted, become no-accounts, made messes of their lives. She knew she was as much to blame as anyone, but she had tried. How could they treat her this way when she had tried so hard?

His mother looked old. In fact, she didn't look well. She seemed distracted, maybe upset about something. What could he say that she would remember after he was gone? It would have to be something that wouldn't hurt her and yet wouldn't seem later to have been a lie.

"Actually, what I came over for was to get a merry Christmas from you."

She stared. "You want me to wish you a—?"

"No, I mean I just figured if I could come and see my ma it would be a merry Christmas for me. Kinda selfish, I guess."

Now what she felt *was* sentiment. What a wonderful thing to hear! What a strange thing for him to say! It was not like him to be emotional or even expressive. "I don't think you're selfish," she said. She wanted to add, "You sure have been over the years, buddy, and what am I supposed to think when I never hear from you?" But she didn't. If being with her was what he wanted for Christmas, that was easy.

She couldn't resist pushing it a little, the compliment had felt so good. "Why do I make it a merry Christmas?"

She had pushed too far. She could see it in his eyes. She lost his gaze. He was self-conscious. His response was edged. "I don't know! Because you're my ma, that's all."

"Well," she said, "I hafta admit, you're the best thing that's happened to me all night."

"Why?"

She shrugged. She didn't want to get into it. Was there something on his mind? Some real reason for his visit? Did he need cash? She wouldn't have given him a dime if she had a hundred bucks. Which she didn't.

Evangeline gazed at him and remembered the night he had come screaming from her loins, a precious child born into turmoil. Had he ever had a happy season, a time when family problems didn't cloud his eyes? She didn't even know what to ask him anymore to simply make conversation. Like her, his spouses and his children were painful subjects.

"I'm glad you came," she tried. "I needed to see one of my children this Christmas." So there it was, she had said it. She had indicted them all, even him. Did he catch it? She couldn't tell. She began to fidget. In some ways she wanted to touch him, to embrace him, to comfort him if he needed her. In another way, she wanted him to go so she could be about her business, the business of finality.

She needs me? he thought. It was the last thing he expected to hear. Now that was a complicator. Needed was something he hadn't felt for he couldn't remember how long. What did she need him for? So she could see one of her children? *One of her* children. *I'm one of her* children. It was a curious word for a middle-aged drunk about to do away with himself. It jarred him. *I am a child. Her child. Someone will miss me.*

"Whatcha drinkin'?" he asked, to break the tension.

"Bouillon, but it's cold."

"I don't mind," he said, reaching for it. "'Slong as it's wet."

But his mother snatched it from his hand, making it slosh. "I've already drunk from it," she lied, "and I have a cold."

Evangeline took it to the kitchen, shaken. Wouldn't that have been a sorry way to go, poisoned by your own mother's suicide potion? She sniffed it. No odor but the bouillon. He would never be able to tell, even if there was residue on his jacket. But what would he think when he heard what had killed her?

What had made her so jumpy? Lefty had no idea. When she asked from the kitchen if he wanted her to make a fresh cup for him, he said no. "I gotta get going soon." This was becoming all too typically awkward. They hadn't interacted as mother and son since he was in elementary school. Too much had been said and done over the years. Nothing would ever be the same. His plan was best. He needed to get on with it.

He was going? She had just gotten used to the idea that he might stay a while. But no, this was OK. All right. She still had her cup. She had betrayed nothing. It would still look like an accident. Twenty minutes ago she wouldn't have guessed he'd have cared. "Well, OK, good-bye then," she said, returning to the living room.

Lefty had expected her to protest. He cocked his head, realizing she accepted his farewell, and stood. He zipped his coat and moseyed to the door. "Thanks for coming," his mother said. "It meant a lot to me."

"Well, I'm glad, but as I say, I came for me."

That meant more to Evangeline than she could say, so she didn't try. He looked so forlorn, so sad, standing there. Because of her decision to take her own life, she was unsure where she would stand with God. That bothered her a whole lot less than wondering about Luschel and his future.

"You goin' to church anywhere?" she said.

He shook his head. "Not for a long time."

She wanted to urge him to go, but that approach had never worked. She wanted to recommend First Church, because though it was big and a little impersonal, he might like it. But she couldn't play mother to him still, not now. It was way too late. Maybe if he thought he was doing it for her? No, he'd see through that. But what if she could just tell him about it somehow? If she mentioned it, and then he found out she was dead, maybe he would remember and go there, out of sentiment.

"I like my church," she said. "But I can't go in the winter when it's so cold and icy."

"Bus stop still six blocks away?"

She nodded. "Could you give me a ride some time? I haven't been in a while." She hated herself for pretending she would even be alive Sunday, but if it got him into church . . .

She felt such a hypocrite. The world would be better off without her, she decided. Lying to get her son back to church!

His mom, the only real Christian in the family, can't even get out to church? After the way they'd treated her all these years, nobody was around to give her a ride? He knew what he had to do. He would leave a note that she should be given his car. It wasn't much, but it would be something.

Then it hit him. That car would be a mess that could never be cleaned up. He would have to do this outside the car, standing in the cold in the middle of nowhere. That was no way to die. But what kind of thinking was that? Who cared? He was going crazy, a fading loser in the middle of the night, trying to leave his mother's house so he could go kill himself.

Why not leave life and his mother with a ray of hope, something for her to go on? Sure, she'd resent him for it in the morning when the awful news came, but it would give her a temporarily merry Christmas.

"Tell you what, Ma. You need a ride to church, you tell me. I'll take ya. I'm not promisin' I'll go in or nothin'. But I'll get you there."

She began to weep. "You'd do that for me?"

He looked away. "I said I would, didn't I?"

He needs me! she decided. *He came here for himself because he needs me!*

"Pick me up Sunday morning," she said, knowing she couldn't say that and follow through with her plan. She would have to flush the deadly bouillon down the toilet.

She needs me, he realized. He could see it written all over her.

"I'll be here," he said.

And as he moved carefully back across the street he noticed the snow had stopped. The sky was clear, the stars illuminating the blanketed ground. He turned to wave at his mother.

Luschel Lefty Boyle drove to an abandoned bridge and dropped that ugly old .44 into the icy water. And then he surprised himself. Without even removing it from the sack, he tossed the expensive pint in too.

He was still a no-account loser, and he wasn't sure he would ever be anything else. But he couldn't go through with his scheme, because his mother needed him. And for once in his life, he would be there.

RICH MAN,
POOR MAN

This time Waylon White was not going to take it. "I always smile and say the best man won, June," he told his wife, "but we both know why he won."

Ralph Kaiser had out-polled Waylon in a congregational vote to finish the term of a recently-deceased deacon. But Ralph was already Sunday school superintendent, and he had been on the youth pastor search committee.

"They always go with the rich guys," June agreed. "Face it."

"Well, I'm gonna hafta tell people what I know about *Mister* Kaiser."

He had her attention. "Like what, hon?"

"Like today, he comes toolin' into the station in that *Benz* of his, rolls up to self-serve and just sits there. I know he usually likes me to fill it and check the oil, do the windows, all that. He just loves havin' me wait on him, ya know."

"Oh, *I* know."

"Well, I sit in the station. I got paperwork to do, too. He may be able to hire people for his red tape work, but I can't. Pretty soon I see him turnin' around in his seat, lookin' for me. I just sit there. I'm wonderin' if he's gonna blow his horn. He'da done that I'da been out there in a second, givin' him a piece of my mind. I don't need that, bein' summoned to the self-serve pump by a honk."

"Did he honk?"

"Nope. Lucky for him. I'da made him wait even longer."

"I thought you said you'd get out there and tell him off."

"Well, I woulda done somethin'. I don't have to take that, 'specially from a brother."

"A brother!" June spat.

"Well, he claims to be a brother in the Lord. But no other brother I know wears a diamond on his pinkie and on a pin through his tie. I wonder how long it'll be before he's got one in his ear!"

"So, what happened?"

"He finally gets out and leans that big body over the roof, peerin' into the station. I stare right at him, but I don't think he can see me from the glare in the window. Finally I mosey on out there and ask him if he needs somethin'. 'Just the usual,' he says."

"The nerve!"

"Yeah! Standin' there at the cheap pump, expectin' me to shuffle and jive for him for four cents less a gallon. He may not have any trouble makin' his margin with all those trucks, but I won't make mine by givin' services away."

"You didn't do it, did you?" his wife said.

"I says, 'You want the fill, the oil, and the windows?' and I say it sorta meaningful like, hopin' he'll catch my drift. He says, 'Yessir, and I appreciate it, Way!' I hate when he calls me that."

"Does he know?"

"He oughta know. Anyway, I make a big production out of doin' all the stuff for him, and he tells me again why he wouldn't mind pumpin' the gas himself but how he hates to go into meetings smellin' of gasoline. It's all right for me, I guess, but not for Mr. Big Shot."

"The gall!"

"It gets worse, June. He tells me that anyway he wants me to make a little more when he comes in, that we businessmen need to help each other."

"You're kidding!"

Waylon held up his left hand and put his right over his heart. "I swear. He says he knows profit is the name of the game in my business as well as his, and then he starts tellin' me again what a nice station I run. Man, that gets me!"

"So patronizing."

"Like there's somethin' big to keepin' a station up. 'Course I hose down the pavement every night, and 'course we keep the bathrooms clean. Yeah, I try to keep the place up, 'cause if I don't I lose my franchise. Those compliments just roll off my back."

"Mine too. Like telling a ditch digger that he sure digs good."

"Exactly. So I finish up, and I tell him how much."

"You charged him full price, I hope."

"I couldn't!"

"Oh, Waylon!"

"Well, what could I do? I didn't wanna embarrass the man, and—"

"No matter how he treats you?"

"I know. So, I tell him the price, and he says, 'Oh, Way'—I hate when he calls me that—"

"Me too."

"'—there has to be some mistake.' I tell him, no, that's what the *self*-serve pump says. And I say it just like that."

June laughed. "You didn't!"

"I absolutely did. Well, that got him, mister. He says, 'Oh, Waylon, no! My mistake!' He's lookin' at the pumps and the signs. 'How could I do that?' he says. I tell him I don't know, and I'm smilin' at him. He says, 'Figure it right for me, Way.'"

"Ooh," June said.

"'—and of course I'll pay you the full amount.' Truth is, acourse, he always, and I mean always, pays with plastic anyway, so—"

"So you might's well be sellin' to him at self-serve prices anyway."

"Yeah, 'cept then I'd lose even more. Anyway, I tell him it would be more trouble to figure it right 'cause I'd have to change the register, put in a make-up slip and all that—which I think he knew in the first place."

"So he just let it ride?"

"He offered me an extra five in cash."

June stared. "He did?"

"Don't get changin' your mind about him, now. He knew I wouldn't take it."

"You didn't take it!?"

"I tried not to. I tell him, 'Hey, cuz,'—I call him that 'cause I think maybe it bugs him the way him callin' me Way always bugs me—"

"He ever tell you that?"

"No. Matter of fact, he almost seems to like it when I call him other names. You know how he seems to beam when people at church call him Big Ralph."

"Yeah."

"I gotta quit doin' that. Anyway, I say to him, 'Cuz,' I says, 'I'm happy to do it,' and then, like I'm kiddin', I punch him in the shoulder, and I say, 'Just don't let it happen again!' I kinda scowl at him, then I laugh real hard like I was teasin'.'"

"Only you weren't."

"'Course I wasn't. You kiddin'? Guy rips me off like that? He insists I take the fin, so I take it."

"Good for you."

"Shoot, yeah."

Waylon stood, proud of himself, and dug the five from his coveralls. He tugged at both ends and made it snap. "Oughta put that on my wall. It's about double the extra he shoulda paid me for full serve."

"Don't feel a bit guilty about it."

"You bet I won't. That guy . . . "

"So, what're you gonna tell people about Ralph to keep 'em from votin' him into all the stuff at church?"

"Well, maybe that story for starters. Everybody sees him as this big, generous, rich guy, but I can see through him a mile away."

"In a New York minute."

"Shoot, yeah. Loves to drive that car to church."

"We paid less for our house."

"Don't I know it. But he was on the missions committee, June. How can a guy be on the missions committee when he'll spend as much on a car as three missionaries could live on in a year?"

"You could feed a small country for what he paid for that thing."

Waylon shook his head and went to take his shower.

That night at the deacon meeting, Ralph Kaiser was largely

silent. Of course, he was large no matter what he did, being a generously proportioned man with a huge face and a loud voice. With a full head of white, wavy hair, he was an imposing figure in expensive suits—which he wore to work and to church, or in the latest fashion casual clothes—which he wore to meetings.

The rest of the deacons tried to include him, to draw him into discussions, but he was reluctant. "If you gentlemen don't mind," he said, "I'd prefer to just listen this first time. I've not been a deacon before, and these matters seem so personal."

"Does that bother you?" one of the men asked.

"Frankly, it does."

"You didn't expect that, Ralph?"

"I guess I did. I'm still not comfortable with the idea of knowing this much about the people I worship with."

"Neither are we, and of course everything in this room stays right here."

"Of course," Ralph said. "I wasn't implying anything. I knew this was an important job, but I have to tell you, I want to come even more prayed up next time."

Several of the men smiled and nodded.

The next week, Waylon White began his campaign against Ralph Kaiser. "Have you ever noticed," he asked a plumber friend, "how the boards—not your committees now, but your important boards—are mostly made up of white collar guys?"

"No, that true?"

"Think about it. Not too many blue collar guys makin' decisions. We're only good for work days and trustee boards. When they really need somethin' done, somethin' requirin' manual labor, they call us."

The plumber nodded. "Asked me to fix some pipes in the downstairs bathroom last spring."

"There you go."

"'Course, what else would they ask me to do, keep the books? Ha!"

"You could keep the books, Mike. You run a tight little business there."

"Well, so do you, Waylon. So how about you?"

"That's just it. They never ask me."

"They asked you to run for deacon, didn't they? I voted for ya."

"Well, thanks. But I didn't make it, did I? Guess I didn't bring enough money to the table."

"That's somethin' I'd never be able to do."

"Be a deacon?"

"No, bring any money to the table!"

That evening Waylon told June of the conversation.

"It was nice he voted for you," she said.

Waylon snorted. "Yeah, but can you imagine a plumber tellin' me he's short of cash? Those guys are rollin' in it. I shoulda been a plumber."

"You sure save us money doing ours."

"Shoot, yeah."

After the deacon meeting, Ralph Kaiser asked to meet with the pastor. "I won't keep you long," he promised.

"Everybody's asleep by now at my place," Pastor Nigel Ingle told him. "Don't rush."

When they were settled in the pastor's study, Ralph told Nigel how surprised he was to have been voted in as a deacon. "I knew Clint well, and frankly, I've never put myself in his category."

Nigel nodded. "Not many people were in his category. He was an unusually selfless and spiritual man."

"Well, that's how I see Waylon."

The pastor raised his brows and said nothing. Ralph continued.

"I mean, every time I go to his station he's got a smile and a kind word. He keeps the place so nice and seems like a real servant. You know, I pulled to the wrong pump the other day and found myself getting irritated that he didn't run right out and serve me like usual. Isn't that just like us selfish humans? Well, he finally realized the mistake was mine, so he came out and treated me like he always does. A smile, a joke. When I realized my mistake he almost wouldn't let me pay him. Made me glad I had voted for him for deacon."

"You voted against yourself?"

Ralph nodded. "I didn't consider it a vote against me. I felt led to accept the nomination, but I didn't have any feeling I was supposed to win. *Win* is the wrong word, of course. I was perfectly happy to run as part of my responsibility and service to the church. But I would have been thrilled if Waylon would have been God's choice."

"Forgive a pastor for being overly spiritual sounding, Ralph, but I tend to trust the sovereignty of the Lord in situations like this. I believe He works through His people. When a congregation votes for a deacon, God has His hand in the result, whether it's close or not. It doesn't have to be unanimous. I believe it's God's will. Don't ask me for chapter and verse."

"I trust the Lord's will in matters like this, too, Pastor, but I can't explain the nagging feeling that it should have been Waylon who was elected."

The pastor leaned back, making his chair squeak. With his hands behind his head, he looked to the ceiling. "Perhaps the Lord was honoring the fact that you were not seeking a position of leadership. I think it was A. W. Tozer who said the only person qualified for leadership is the one who feels inadequate. I've taken liberties with the quote, but you get the point."

Ralph fell silent. "Pastor," he said finally, "if feeling inadequate qualifies me, I'm eminently qualified."

Nigel smiled. "OK then? Feel better? Gonna stick with it?"

"I guess. But I'm also going to push to get Waylon White more involved, maybe on committees or something. That guy ought to be a greeter at least."

The pastor changed the subject. "Stop telling yourself you're not qualified, now. You've visited missionaries overseas, have entertained full-time staff candidates in your home, and though by policy I don't know the details, I know you've been generous to the church."

Ralph was embarrassed. "You may recall I made a recommitment to the Lord a few years ago."

"I do."

"I was dead serious, Pastor. It wasn't that I was away from Him before that, but I had never really jumped into the game."

"Well, you sure have since."

"To His glory," Ralph said. "I know how trite that sounds, but I meant business. I want the Lord to have all of me."

"That's the kind of a man I want on the deacon board, Ralph. Take your election as from the Lord, and get busy."

A month later the deacons discussed a business owner in the church, Jennie McCullers, who had been accused of hiring irregularities. Miss McCullers was under indictment by the government, and board members wanted to be in a position to take disciplinary action or to stand by her, depending on what they themselves found.

One of the men suggested that they send in a team of independent consultants. "We can't go disciplining someone just because a disgruntled former employee or two have something against her."

"We need to talk to her, too, don't we?" Ralph said.

"Yes," the chairman said, "but she has already gone on record that she has an attorney and that on his advice she will be stonewalling the government hiring commission."

"You think she'll stonewall us, too?" Ralph said.

"'Fraid so," the chairman said.

Ralph frowned. "Serious accusation."

"I know, but she's a tough cookie. We want to avoid besmirching the reputation of the church."

"And the Lord," Ralph said, sounding more pious than he intended.

"Of course."

Ralph had an idea. "Let's appoint a subcommittee with, say, just one deacon and a couple from the congregation at large."

"I like the idea of getting a wife involved," someone said. "How about your wife, Ralph?"

"She'd be good," he said, "but I was thinking that the couple should both be members at large, and the committee chair should be a deacon. Maybe you, Harv."

Harvey smiled and looked at the others, who smiled also. "Do you all agree that *Ralph's* idea is a good one?" he asked in meaningful tones. Ralph wasn't sure where this was leading.

"Yes," they all joined in aloud. "*Ralph's* idea *is* a good one."

"Do we need to vote on *Ralph's* idea?"

"No," several said. "Consensus! Consensus!"

Had they not been smiling, Ralph would have thought he had committed a major faux pas. Why were they emphasizing his name?

The chairman called for order. "Now, Ralph," he said, "let me explain. We have a long-standing policy here. We look for good ideas like yours, and when one arises, our work is half done. We like it, we approve it by consensus, and we assign it to the person who came up with it."

"In other words," Ralph said, "I'm going to chair the subcommittee."

"You are."

Ralph grinned as if he'd been had.

"Of course," the chairman continued, "if you'd really, seriously rather not, we won't force you."

"No," Ralph said. "I'm willing. I wouldn't want to violate any traditions. Would you approve my choices for committee members?"

"You're ready?"

"If you are."

"Proceed."

"Waylon and June White."

There was no comment and no motion. Ralph took that as tacit approval.

The next day after work, Ralph stopped at Waylon's filling station. "I was wondering if you and your wife would have time to chat with me this evening."

"Sure, what about?"

"I'd rather wait to get into it. Should I drop by, or would you like to come to our place?"

"You can come over," Waylon said. As soon as Ralph was out of sight, Waylon phoned home and told his wife.

"June," he concluded, "somethin's up."

"Why would a fat cat like that want to come to our little place?" she said. "Just to make us feel bad? You shoulda told him we'd come there."

"Are you kiddin'? Mansion like that would give me the willies. I wouldn't even know what to do. Just get the place cleaned up, 'cause he's comin'."

"What do you think he wants, hon?"

"I don't know. I just hope nobody squealed on me for bad-mouthin' him."

"Your home is as lovely as your station," Ralph said as he settled into the worn, foam rubber couch. This, he was convinced, was a humble couple who cared about their surroundings and their image. The children were upstairs and fairly quiet, and the place and the Whites seemed freshly scrubbed. *This is the kind of a guy I wouldn't mind having in my company,* Ralph thought.

He was, however, puzzled by the Whites' reaction to his request. They tried to turn down his appointment to the subcommittee, which gave him only more confidence to proceed. The pastor had said that Ralph's reluctance actually made him a better servant, so that had to be true of the Whites as well.

They seemed to genuinely not want to get involved, but Ralph insisted. Mrs. White pleaded that she knew nothing of business or laws or ethics, but Ralph assured her that her main role was to provide balance. Waylon said he was more comfortable doing hands-on, manual labor type stuff. "Give me a floor to wax or a wall to paint," he said with a sheepish grin.

"Oh, you've done plenty of that, and there'll always be more of that to do," Ralph said, liking this humble man more the more he got to know him. "I'll really appreciate your meeting with Jenny McCullers and me. I'll speak with her this evening to set the stage, and I'll call you about when she can get together with the three of us. Thank you both."

When he prayed with them before leaving, he sensed they were still reluctant and upset. He knew they would feel more comfortable after they'd had time to think, just as he had after talking with the pastor.

As soon as Ralph was gone, headed for Jennie McCullers's office, June and Waylon turned to each other.

"What're we gonna do, babe?" he said.

"Get her on the phone quick."

Waylon called her home and got an answering machine. "Jenny, call Waylon or June as soon as possible. It's urgent. You have our number."

He turned to his wife. "What's her office number?"

"Our offices are closed," the business machine said. "Please call back, Monday through Friday, between the hours of—"

He slammed down the phone. "We've got to get over there. She's probably workin' late, but the switchboard's closed."

"I can't get a babysitter on this short a notice, Waylon. You go."

"I just hope Kaiser thinks she's home and goes there first."

But he hadn't. When Waylon screeched around the corner in his tow truck, he saw the *Mercedes* in the parking lot and the light on in Jennie McCullers's office. *Oh, no!*

Ralph Kaiser was warmly welcomed by Miss McCullers. He was impressed with the size of her manufacturing company and said so. She was cautiously receptive until Ralph got to the point of his call. "The deacon board has assigned a subcommittee, and we'd like to set up an appointment with you to discuss your problem."

"I am under counsel not to talk about it," she said coldly. "And I certainly wouldn't want the church poking its nose into my affairs."

Ralph grew serious. "Our intention is to help. I won't kid you and say that if we found any of the accusations true we wouldn't have to discuss eventualities, but our hope—"

"Your hope! That's a laugh! Your hope is to help me out of this mess? Your hope is to get as much distance between the church and me as you can, so when my house of cards comes down, you won't look bad."

"That's not what we have in mind, ma'am, unless you're implying that there is something fragile here that's about to give way."

"Nothing more than is under your own roof, Kaiser."

"I beg your pardon."

"I've heard plenty about you."

"About me?"

"Don't act so innocent. I see how you flaunt your wealth, and I know how you step on the little guy, how you treat the blue collar workers."

"I'm not here to defend myself," Ralph said, but he couldn't stop himself. "Let me tell you that my drivers are paid so well and have benefits so attractive that they don't even belong to a union."

"I'm not talking about your own employees, sir. I'm talking about the people you call your friends. The people you call your brothers."

Ralph was stunned. He might have expected defensiveness, but this was an attack. What was she driving at? "I'm not following you," he admitted.

"Of course you're not! You're blind to your own boorishness. You treat the little guy like dirt, you rub his nose in it, you patronize him, you wear your diamonds and drive your fancy cars, and you can't imagine you have an enemy in the world."

"Who are you talking about, ma'am? If I've offended someone, I want to make it right. It might sound strange to you, but your being a successful businesswoman, you certainly understand: I actually live *below* my means. We could afford to live in a much nicer home and have several new models of the older car we drive."

"The older *Mercedes!* How big of you!"

"If I thought that car offended you, I'd—"

"Me? You think I'd be offended by a *Mercedes?* What do you think *I* drive?"

"Then whom am I offending?"

"You really don't know, do you?"

"Please tell me." Ralph couldn't believe he had got himself into this position. He hadn't wanted to explain himself and allow the spotlight to drift from her. One thing he would have trouble believing now was that she was innocent. She sounded like someone who *would* discriminate in hiring, not pay minimum wage, and be generally unfair in her employment practices. She certainly didn't sound like the believers he knew well at First Church. She was no Waylon or June White, that was for sure.

"You park that car in the church lot, and you—"

"In the back, yes. The only reason people might notice is that we come early. I'm Sunday school—"

"Superintendent, I know. Everybody knows. You've got all the power positions. No one who really wants to serve can do a thing at that church because of people like you."

"I'd gladly step aside—"

"Oh, sure you would. That car is prominent, your suits scream extravagance—"

"They're expensive, but they're half what my colleagues pay. How many men in my position do you know who buy their suits off the rack?" He hated himself for explaining.

"Six-figure men, you mean?"

Of course he was a six-figure man, but he certainly wasn't going to get into that.

"If there's something I've done that has somehow—"

"Oh, Kaiser, don't start with your humble routine. You may get away with that on your deacon board and your search committee and your missions committee, but don't think you can—"

Ralph was stunned. How did she know so precisely what his positions were at the church? He was feeling ill, but he had run into personalities like this before. He would not buckle, but he wouldn't get into a street fight either. He had to know what she was saying and for whom she was speaking. Who were these little people so incensed by his visibility?

He felt the color and anger rising in him and wanted to defend himself, but he also wanted to do the job he was sent to do.

"Let me ask you something, Miss McCullers. Are you or are you not willing to meet with the subcommittee of the deacon board to explain the charges against you and either get our help or submit to our authority?"

"I thought I had made myself more than clear," she said. "I am not interested in any subcommittee made up of you and others like you. I thought that church would be a good place for contacts, but you and the rest are nitpickers. I wouldn't even want to try to get you in my corner."

It was time to pull out his ace. He hadn't intended to withhold the fact that two-thirds of the subcommittee was made up of a blue-collar couple. His not mentioning it had been providential, though, he thought. Had she known of the Whites' involvement she would have been hard-pressed to make the charges she'd made. A man who had handpicked Waylon and June could not be the ogre she made him out to be, regardless who else thought so.

"It might interest you to know that Waylon and June White make up the rest of the subcommittee," he said. He couldn't deny he was delighted to see the shock register on her face. He was puzzled, however, by her laugh.

She threw her head back and guffawed from her depths. "The Whites?!"

Don't even think of trying to besmirch their reputations, he thought. *I will tolerate an attack on me, but not on people like that.*

"The Whites?" she repeated. "If they volunteered for this duty, they must—"

"They didn't volunteer. I personally selected them."

She laughed again. "You fool, Kaiser. You would be blind enough to choose them. Where do you think I heard all I just said about you? If they *had* volunteered, they'd have been playing both ends against the middle! I can imagine how they tried to squirm out of this responsibility!"

Ralph Kaiser trudged from his driveway to his home a sadder and wiser man. Two months later, when Jennifer McCullers was found guilty of discrimination, the church was left with no action. She had withdrawn her membership within hours after her meeting with Ralph.

Because so many parishioners came forward to complain about the Whites' bad-mouthing of Ralph Kaiser, the church did take disciplinary action against them. To their credit Waylon and June repented of their jealousy and their gossip and asked to be restored. Ralph wept with many others when he heard their confession. He wished the Whites hadn't avoided him after the meeting. He bore them no ill will.

Some lessons, he decided, were repulsive and painful. But he was grateful for one thing: as he parked his used Oldsmobile in the garage he breathed a prayer of thanks that he had learned as much about himself as he had about others, difficult as that had been to face.

MR. MINISTRY

L ater Nigel Ingle would attribute his trauma to stress and fatigue. But as is common in such cases, he was unaware of those maladies at the time.

He knew he was tired, of course, maybe even into what the experts called sleep deprivation. That was nothing new. Nigel was a man who loved his work. He was not a workaholic, had not—his wife assured him—deprived his family for the sake of First Suburban. At least for several years.

He had to admit that at first his priorities had indeed been skewed. He had come to this community having seen two small congregations double in size and begin building programs. He was a forward-thinking man, a people person, and people loved to hear him preach. His heart and soul were in the pastorate.

When he arrived at First Church six years before, he had a young family. He and Jennifer were raising three great kids, two girls and a boy. Or he should say, Jennifer was raising them. He was big into "quality time" back then. Quantities of time was something he simply didn't have.

The search committee that hired him had assured him they didn't expect the same results he'd had in his first two pastorates. That was intended to be reassuring. "You may have been able to see seventy-five grow to one-fifty and then see a hundred-and-ten grow to two-and-a-quarter, and maybe those little churches needed new buildings, but that's not what we're looking for."

They were kidding themselves, of course. He knew it, and they knew it. Both he and the committee talked for hours about how numbers weren't important, that what they really wanted for their nearly three hundred regular attenders was his brand of exciting, expository preaching. "Not many men have the gift of making the verse-by-verse thing come alive. You, son, have got it, and we want it. Don't trouble yourself with expansion and building. We've been through that. We've got a nice facility, and we've got room for more people, but that's not our aim."

They discussed the tragedy of churches becoming too large, rather than reproducing themselves in sister works. They pontificated on pastors burned out through having to do everything themselves. Nigel was assured that he would be expected to put at least half his time into sermon preparation. "You have a staff, and we expect you to use it."

And he had. But there had been an extended period of learning, of getting to know everyone. Nigel used his gifts of discernment and his analytical mind to quickly determine who were the talkers and who were the walkers. He spent hours and hours at the church in meetings and in ministry, until his wife had to get his attention.

Jennifer was a soft-spoken, behind-the-scenes woman who was a help-meet and supporter in the old-fashioned way. She saw no conflict in submitting to her husband's authority and deferring to his spiritual headship. But both were grateful that she was also honest and that she had learned the importance of holding him accountable for certain things.

For instance, he preached and practiced what he called co-submission. Yes, husbands were in positions of headship in their homes, but the Bible also emphasized submitting to one another. "Headship is reserved for loggerheads," he said more than once. "A husband is not to subject his wife; she is to submit herself. And he is to do the same."

That philosophy had improved and saved many a marriage, and it rescued Nigel's. Because the day came when his wife took him up on his openness. She called his secretary and made an appointment with him, asking that Sylvia not say who was coming.

"Oh, a little surprise?" Sylvia said, a smile in her voice.

"Uh-huh."

"I love that," the secretary said. "My late husband was a spontaneous guy, and it's one of my sweetest memories."

"Who's the counselee this morning, Syl?" the pastor said, standing in the doorway with his appointment book in his hand.

"Didn't use a name," she said.

"You know her?"

"Yes, sir."

"Do I?"

"Yes."

"Why the mystery?"

"Guess you'll have to ask her."

"You'll be here when she arrives? You know I like to keep the door open and you nearby."

"I'll be as close as necessary, sir."

Jennifer Ingle was not big on what she and Nigel called PDAs, public displays of affection. But neither was she averse to holding hands or even sneaking a quick peck of greeting. He kidded her that she was territorial and that she shouldn't expect the same in return—"I might look a bit hungrier than is appropriate for a pastor"—but she knew he enjoyed her.

He was thrilled to see her that day and told her so. Because it was just Sylvia and Sue (from the counseling staff) in the office when Jennifer arrived, Nigel didn't even mind embracing his wife when she arrived. The decision to shut the door was hers.

Jennifer was a smart woman. She took an interesting and indirect approach. When Nigel asked where she would like him to sit, she asked him to sit wherever he usually sat when counseling a married woman. With a smirk he returned to the chair behind his desk and pointed her to a chair that faced his.

"May I help you, ma'am?"

"Yes, Pastor. I have a marital problem."

Nigel's smile froze. She had been complaining a little about his time at the office and away from the kids. But generally she had been supportive and loving. He assumed his schedule was a typical pastor's dilemma.

"A problem?"

"Yes, sir. I can't get my husband's attention. He's a caring, attentive man, but I don't think he realizes how serious the problem is."

Nigel's heart raced. What was she trying to say? "Tell me," he said.

"I don't want my marriage and my family to become orbital," she said. "Do you know what I'm saying?"

"I think so."

"I'm not sure my husband understands that," she said to her husband. "When he's home he's great with me and with the kids, but we need more of him. He talks a lot about how important family life and marriage is and how your ministry really can't be effective if you're not ministering at home."

"And you don't think he's ministering at home?"

"We miss him."

Nigel appreciated his wife's getting his attention, but of course he didn't want games like that characterizing their relationship. When she was gone he left his door closed and sat and thought and prayed until it was time to go home. There they talked honestly and openly, and he thanked her for having taken the risk of confronting him.

When he had his priorities in order and his work day narrowed to no more than ten hours, evening meetings included, the church exploded. Nigel felt so much better about himself, so fulfilled by his relationships with Jennifer and the children, that he was freer to go full speed when he was working.

People enjoyed his preaching more than ever. He proved to be a better administrator of a larger staff than he'd ever expected. People enjoyed working with and for him and following him. As a personal witness, he was an example. With careful planning he met with every nonattending member he could find, then started on the nonmembers who had attended within the last couple of years. He became a salesman for the church.

His reading on marketing and meeting the needs of the modern community resulted in agencies and programs the church had never dreamed of. They started an outreach to the needy, to the homeless, to the hungry. They offered counseling and even legal aid. Some of the oldsters wondered aloud if they were becoming a social gospel headquarters with more emphasis on the social than on the gospel. Nigel preached a series of sermons on Jesus' admonitions about His followers' responsibilities to the poor. Then he recruited the critics to be spiritual advisers and to devise ways to ensure that every person who was helped and impacted by the church knew the motivation of the Christians helping them.

People were coming to Christ through all those ministries, and they were becoming members of First Church. The building was jammed on weekends and several nights during the week. Even the staunchest status quo types began making noises about building again. How handy to have a pastor who had been through that before.

Jennifer worried that Nigel was working too hard. "Not too long," she assured him. "Just too hard."

"I can't get enough of it, Jen. It motivates me. If I neglect the family, tell me. Otherwise, I've gotta keep running."

It worked. All of it worked. The church lost a few members who didn't like to see races mixed in Sunday school and church, and a few others who "just don't care for big churches." But with the influx from the community and the new evangelistic fervor of the veteran members, the church grew and grew. The pastor worked hard at not letting the beautiful new building plans interrupt the ministries.

His known enemies were gone, he was at harmony with his boards and his staff, and things were good in his marriage and with his kids. He'd heard the warnings from other leaders about keeping careful monitors on all the areas of one's personal life, so he was keeping in shape spiritually and physically too. If anything, he felt a little guilty about how great everything was going. He knew the folly of measuring success by numbers, and he knew also that every blessing came from God.

There was too much to do to become restless. His task at First Church was far from done. As the years rolled past and his kids grew up, the church reached the seven hundred-member mark, and life was grand. Nigel had found himself drifting from the personal contact with the body he enjoyed so much, but that changed after he found himself forced to personally counsel a troubled member. He was reminded of why he had got into the ministry in the first place, and he began adding to his schedule opportunities to personally interact more with the parishioners. That meant cutting out other things, because he would not over-crowd his schedule again. How grateful he was that he had learned that lesson, from his wife, early enough to make a difference in his own family.

The pastor was in demand as a speaker, but he followed the examples of leaders he knew who, by policy, were away from their own churches on Sundays only when they were on vacation. Even when guest speakers came or other staff members preached (which Nigel encouraged), he was there, visible and supportive.

He was careful to discuss with Jennifer when, where, and how many conference engagements he should accept. When he could, he took the family, or at least individual members, with him.

Nigel Ingle had become a highly visible, successful pastor of a wonderful church. It was not a super- or a mega-church. He had little interest in seeing attendance reach a thousand or two, unless that was what God wanted. He merely wanted to be faithful. Others in his position might be looking for the perfect career opportunity. He believed he was where he was supposed to be, and he was committed to staying for as long as the church wanted him. That, to him, was a gauge of God's approval. When God wanted him to leave, the people would let him know.

He dressed well, drove a nice car, lived comfortably, had a happy and well-adjusted family, and he worked hard. Very hard. He was running at top speed in every area and was unaware of stress. As he liked to tell anyone who wondered, he couldn't be happier or more fulfilled.

What was most gratifying was going to a distant city at someone else's expense, being picked up at the airport by an admiring young person who had read one of his articles or booklets or heard one of his tapes, being put up in a nice hotel or at the home of a wealthy church member, and being free to minister with energy.

What a wonderful bonus, he thought. *A blessing. The servant of the Lord being taken care of by the people he ministered to.* It didn't make him any easier on them in the pulpit. He called the church, his and others, to a life of commitment and service. He challenged them, exhorted them, admonished them. Choose up sides. Get in the game. Sell out. Count the cost. Pay it.

The day came when he pulled into the church parking lot at 6:00 one Sunday morning, as was his custom, and simply sat in his car looking at the facility. It was beautiful. No, that was too pedestrian a word. It was gorgeous. A true monument to God's glory. It was not ostentatious. No one could criticize it for that. The complex was simply tasteful, classy, functional, a feather in the community's cap.

Nigel felt grateful. He had been an instrument of God in seeing this place grow. He thought of the hundreds of homes he had visited, the thousands of people he had spoken to, the boards he had united, the emotions he had soothed. How good it was to be used of God. He had not expected or sought his reward before heaven, but he appreciated the bounty that had come to him as a result of this ministry. He was not ashamed to say he had given it his all, and though he believed he was willing to go anywhere and suffer any hardship for God, he was grateful that God had seen fit to put him here and to reward him for having sold out. Glory to God.

His pattern was to unlock the back door to the main building and pray in his office for an hour before reviewing his sermon. He was a disciplined man, not one to frantically prepare the night before and the morning itself. He considered his sermon preparation done when he could recite his message almost verbatim without notes by Friday afternoon. He ignored it Saturday, prayed over it early Sunday morning—as well as for the people—and reviewed it briefly before taking the pulpit.

What a gift awaited him that morning. In his box was a piece of mail that had come the day before, inviting him to be the keynote speaker at a nationally-known pastor's conference. He was on the program with men who had nationwide radio and television audiences and who had authored best-selling books. It would be a privilege, an honor. And he was the main speaker. His topic was to be "The Local Church in the 21st Century." He could preach that in his sleep, but he would prepare and make it a winner.

By the time of the pastor's conference several months hence, Nigel had been given a generous raise, which he accepted gratefully, admitting that with two children in college now it would be put to good use. The church had urged him to use his auto allowance for an even nicer car, fitting the dignity of his office. After all, he had a reserved parking space, and new people expected to see an appropriate vehicle for the senior pastor. Not extravagant. Just right.

Make no mistake. Much as Nigel enjoyed his station and his work, he was still committed and sold-out. Regardless of the trappings that went with the success of the church and its ministries, he remained active in personal ministry. Admittedly, the sudden accidental death of the chairman of his deacon board made Nigel think about the brevity and the unpredictability of life. But it also gave him one more sermon topic that rang a bell with middle-aged men.

"Do good," Jennifer said in the car at the airport, leaning to kiss him good-bye.

Nigel strode to his gate traveling light, as was his wont. The suit, the shoes, even the bag, were just right. He wanted to be an appropriate ambassador of his church and of his Lord. If the situation presented itself, he would tell his seatmate about his faith. Planes were such good venues for that.

The conference planners had insisted that he fly first class, which he at first told them was unnecessary and then reluctantly accepted. It would be a fun, new experience, and if they insisted . . .

As it turned out, the plane was overbooked and his first-class seatmate turned out to be a pastor on his first plane ride since seminary "when I flew home for my mom's funeral."

The Rev. Danny Dixon introduced himself and began witnessing before Nigel could speak. "Hey, this is something, isn't it? First class. Boy, I didn't expect this. I'm not even dressed for it, know what I mean?"

He laughed. In his polyester double-knits, thin white shirt, and three years out-of-date tie, he did indeed look out of place in first class. Nigel had been sitting there pretending to belong and, he thought, probably succeeding. At least Danny Dixon hadn't guessed him to be a pastor.

"I'm a preacher, I don't mind telling you, and I'm on my way to a pastors' conference. I can't wait. I've wanted to go ever since I got into the ministry twelve years ago, and I'm gonna be hearing guys this week I've only seen on videos or heard on radio. Man, it's gonna be something. I consider myself a PR guy for God, if that makes any sense. He shouldn't need an advance man, but I'm sold on Him and what He can do for people. I won't cram anything down your throat, but if you want to know real life and happiness, get your sins forgiven, and know you're going to heaven, you're talking to the right guy."

Nigel reached to shake his hand, smiling tolerantly at his new friend's enthusiasm and wondering how many unsuspecting prospects he had alienated with that crass, direct approach. "Nigel Ingle," he said, "First Suburban Ch—"

"You don't say! You're Nigel Ingle?" He pumped Nigel's hand. "I read your thing in that magazine about starting a soup kitchen, and do you know our little church—eighty-seven of us and counting—does that two nights a week and sometimes has more hungry people than we have in church on Sundays."

"That's gratifying. Thanks for letting me know."

"Lord's blessed it, Pastor. God's sure used you."

"Thank you."

When they got off the plane, Danny Dixon maintained a running monologue until they had reached the baggage claim and ground transportation area. "Anything I can help you carry?" Danny said.

"No, this is all I brought," Nigel said, showing Danny his garment bag.

"Oh, well, then if you wouldn't mind, I've got a couple of pieces coming I could use a hand with."

"Well, I am expecting to be met."

"Oh, you think I could catch a ride?"

"Um, well, I couldn't speak for the driver, but—"

"Sure, maybe they've got different people coming for the speakers. Oh, here's my trunk now. Could you just help me get it to the curb?"

"Sure."

Nigel grabbed the huge box and nearly stumbled under the weight. "What's in this thing?"

Danny laughed as he lugged two other suitcases. "It's full of Spanish New Testaments. We got too many for our ministry, and there's a work in this town that needs 'em. 'Fact, you could help me take 'em down there tomorrow."

"I'm speaking tomorrow."

"Tomorrow night, right? I'm talking about in the morning."

"Perhaps," Nigel said. "Here comes my ride."

The collegian driving for Nigel rushed to take his garment bag, complimented him on it, shook his hand, and opened the door for him. Danny Dixon approached. "Uh, Pastor Ingle was gonna see if there was room for one more. I'm going to the conference, too."

"I have to pick up two more speakers at another exit, sir," the kid said. "If your name was on the list, just wait here and someone will be by."

"Great! See you, Nigel! Maybe tomorrow, huh?"

"Perhaps."

"You'll love this Spanish ministry!"

Nigel nodded, hoping he might be hard to find the next day. Or at least that there might be some conflicting responsibility.

When Nigel and the two other speakers in his car were delivered to the hotel, each was escorted to his room by a host who made sure he had everything he needed, double-checked that his fruit basket was waiting, and explained how to charge meals and incidentals to the room. As the driver was leaving Nigel's room he received a message on his walkie-talkie. They were short a driver, and there was a group of pastors waiting at the airport.

"Which ones?" Nigel's host asked, checking his list.

"Smith, Dixon, Barnes, Wilson, and Adams," came the staticky reply.

"I'll see what I can do and get back to you," the host said. He looked at Nigel apologetically, and Nigel smiled with sympathy. "Say," the young man said, "that isn't something you could help us with, is it?"

"Me?"

"You know how to get back to the airport, don't you?"

"Well, sure, but—"

"These guys are waiting right where we picked you up. You've met Dixon, and the rest are with him. They've got lots of luggage, but I think you can fit them in the four-door. I really appreciate this."

Nigel could hardly believe it. He hadn't recalled agreeing. And he was counting on some downtime to watch a ball game and recharge before his important message the next evening. He took the keys, trying to hide his disappointment and reluctance. *You'd have thought they could plan better than this,* he told himself. *Having your program people pick up conferees!*

The four-door proved to be a foreign compact, but when Nigel suggested that one or two of the pastors wait for another ride, they all insisted they didn't mind being a little cramped. Danny Dixon's bags filled the trunk, and the rest of the men sat on cases and had luggage on their laps as well. Two pastors wound up in the front seat, forcing Nigel to excuse himself every time he tried to shift gears.

Once they were laboriously under way to the cheaper hotel down the road from Nigel's, Danny Dixon informed everyone who their driver was. There was a chorus of greetings and compliments. Then a voice from the backseat.

"I'm a subscriber to your printed messages, Pastor Ingle," Rev. James Barnes said.

"Thank you."

"You know what has meant the most to me in the last few years?"

"Tell me." Nigel looked in the rearview mirror but could see neither Pastor Barnes nor out the back window over the stack of suitcases.

"You did a message on true success in ministry. Remember it?"

"Refresh me."

"Well, it was about not measuring God's blessing by the size of your church, or your salary, or your position. You said something about there being no upward or downward steps in the ministry. True success, you said, was in knowing you were doing what God wanted you to do, no matter what the results."

Nigel nodded, color in his cheeks.

"I have to tell you, at first that bothered me. I saw your picture on the booklet and the aerial shot of your church, and I read that little paragraph about all the people and all the ministries you have there. I found myself thinking, *Sure, that's easy for him to say.* I mean if I was somebody important and well-known and successful in everybody's eyes, I'd be able to preach about how none of that makes any difference."

Nigel squirmed.

"But then I read between the lines," Barnes continued, "and the Lord really convicted me about my attitude. I could tell you were the kind of a guy who meant what he said. At first I thought that was why God had blessed you with such obvious success, but then I realized that you would have preached the same message and been just as right if you were in my situation."

Nigel was glad for the chance to change the subject. "And your situation is?"

"We meet in a school. There are about twenty core families. We're in a depressed and changing neighborhood, a genteel way of saying it's mixed. We're a success though, because we're doing what God called us to do."

"Reaching out to your community, are you?" Nigel said.

"Yes, sir."

"Good for you."

The mention of outreach brought Danny Dixon back into the conversation. He excitedly told the others about his cache of New Testaments and how he and Nigel were going to be distributing them in a Spanish area the next morning. Nigel rolled his eyes, hoping no one noticed.

"Really?" Barnes said, "Can I get in on that?"

"Me too," the others chimed in. "What time?"

"Maybe one of you can take my place," Nigel said. "I have a lot of preparing to do."

"You don't want to miss out on that, do you, Pastor Ingle?" one of the others said.

"There's plenty of work for all of us," Dixon said. "Don't miss the blessing," he added, looking at Nigel.

"Look," Nigel said angrily, surprising even himself, "I'm here to serve as a speaker and to get a little break. I've already done my bit by being pressed into service as a driver and a baggage handler. Now I will not be able to join you. I'm sorry."

The others looked away and at each other in embarrassed silence.

"I'll be praying for you," Nigel added lamely.

"Well," Dixon said, clearing his throat. "We appreciate that. We need all the prayer we can get."

Nigel went back to his hotel humiliated. He envied the zeal of those humble pastors who had come away for a time of fun and relaxation and inspiration and yet could think of nothing they'd rather do than personally minister in a hard area. What an example he had been to them!

He did not sleep well that night, and early in the morning he awoke in shame. He tried to pray and found himself spiritually paralyzed. As he lay there, trying to enjoy his position of privilege, he was disgusted with himself. Over and over in his mind played the memory of trying to separate himself from pedestrian pastors he had actually considered beneath him. He had been reluctant to get involved in real ministry. What had happened to him?

He slid off the bed and knelt before God, his face on the floor. At 7:00 he called Danny Dixon at his hotel.

"How are we getting where we're going?"

"Excuse me?"

"I'm coming with you."

"Great! The Spanish pastor has an old van. He's picking us up at eight-fifteen."

"I'll be there. And tell the others I'm bringing over some fruit for breakfast."

"Great!"

"As for me, I will eat my words from yesterday."

After a long pause, Dixon said, "The men will be very happy to have you with us."

Nigel found himself choked up as he apologized for his outburst. The other pastors embraced him and then, to his relief, forgot the incident.

The gratitude on the faces of the Spanish pastor and the people in his community affected Nigel in a way he could hardly compute. He knew he would not be the same man, the same pastor he had been. It also changed the message he preached that night.

He said basically the same words he had prepared, but he added the personal story of his initial reluctance to get down and dirty in ministry on a trip that was designed with ministry in mind. He wanted nothing personal standing in the way if the Lord urged him to call the entire assemblage of pastors to rededication.

He wasn't about to challenge fellow pastors from all levels of the church to renewed commitment to personal ministry, unless he himself had learned the lesson. He would never again tell ministers that success should not be measured in terms of numbers and visibility until he quit doing that himself.

Nigel told his story with honesty, vulnerability, and most of all, true humility. The place was deathly silent as he told of his own deep conviction the night before. He was not trying to manipulate anyone or play mind games. When he asked his compatriots to indicate their desire to recommit themselves to personal ministry he wished with all his heart that he was in the congregation rather than on the platform. He would have loved to have raised his hand, to come forward, to kneel and pray.

Many responded, and Nigel was as emotional as they.

When his plane finally touched down, he looked forward to telling Jen what had happened in his life. God had met him and rescued him from the brink of a spiritual disaster, of which he had not even been aware.

THE ALMIGHTY DEAL

B ernard Ulysses Kinney was out of his field, but he knew a good thing when he saw one. By trade, Bernie was a life insurance salesman. His company encouraged him to call himself an estate planner, and even provided for him a monthly newsletter—with his name imprinted at the top—to send to prospects and clients.

Bernie was good at his job, friendly and efficient. Most of all, he was tireless. He would make no fewer than twenty cold calls a day. He liked to dress well and eat well and live comfortably, and he was married to a woman newly used to that lifestyle. She had embraced it with all her being. Tiffany (she went by Taffy) Kinney found ways of working into conversations the latest projects around her huge home.

Taffy frequently mentioned that their "second" car was hers. It was a luxury car most families only dream of. Her husband's, of course, was even nicer. Taffy bragged under the guise of complaining.

"You can never trust those finicky German transmissions," she'd say. "Bernie's having the same trouble with his. I don't know why we bother." Then she'd add, conspiratorially, "Of course mechanics see that car and the cash register starts ringing. They're supposed to last forever and all that, but they cost an arm and a leg every time we turn around."

The next week she would complain about how expensive interior decorators were. "It didn't seem to be this high last year when we repainted."

People guessed that the Kinneys were living beyond their means. What they owned was what anyone with a higher than average income could have if they were willing to live in debt. It was worth it to Bernie and Taffy to juggle their credit cards and cut corners on certain things so they would appear wealthier than they were. Only the First Suburban treasurer knew that their only contributions to the church were the occasional twenties Bernie dropped into the plate.

It wasn't that they didn't claim to be believers. They were even active in church in their unique ways. Bernie wasn't much for work days or running a kids' program, and no one had ever heard him give a devotional or even pray in public. But he would provide the food for a picnic or rent a van for an outing. He might even drive.

It nagged friends that the Kinneys didn't entertain much and didn't often seem available to be entertained either. They were nice enough. Taffy might speak with you for fifteen minutes or even a half hour, and later you realized that everything she said had centered around herself. Her life. Her house. Her car. Her kids. Her husband. You might have been reminded of

110

something your own little darling had said or done, but when you worked it into the conversation it became an orphaned thought, a mere reminder of another Taffy story.

Bernie was better, but his patter was all surface. You got the feeling he had been trained to keep the spotlight on the other guy so he would feel good about himself and about Bernie. Bottom line, it was a sales gimmick. "How are things in your life?" he would begin, with a slap on the back or a warm, pumping, elbow-grabbing handshake.

He didn't really want to know about your spiritual life, your doubts, fears, struggles, inconsistencies, or bad news. He merely wanted you to talk about what was supposed to please you most—yourself. And usually it worked. If you told him six years ago that your nine year old was thrilled with his first Little League home run, Bernie would never forget it. That kid might have never hit another or even played baseball again. He might play piccolo in the high school band now. But Bernie would bring up that homer every time he greeted you. "How ya doin'? And the wife? She still gardening?" (She might have died in the meantime.) "And how's Junior, the slugger?"

"He's enjoying high school, Bern."

"Bet he's still knocking 'em out of here, huh?"

"Not really."

"Don't be modest now. Kid's gonna make you rich someday!"

Getting rich someday, really rich, occupied a great deal of Bernie Kinney's mind. When people asked him what he was up to, if he was staying busy, or how the life insurance business was going, he always implied he had something else in the works. He used clichés such as "bigger fish to fry," "other irons in the fire," and "chasing another rainbow."

His wife wanted a mink. And a Hawaiian vacation. Maybe a trip to Europe. And the kids. Surely they wouldn't have to go to some ordinary state university. Even if they weren't Ivy League material, private colleges were the only options. Bernie loved his lifestyle but not his debt load. His schemes and plans never included cutting his outgo. They always involved increasing his income. And though he had somehow managed to steadily increase his income every year, his and his wife's spending was always up to the challenge. He never got ahead. He never even stayed level. He slipped further and further behind until his debt tripled his annual income.

Bernie was a rationalizer, and that saved him from an early grave. A more realistic man, less of a dreamer, would have done one of two things: worried himself sick and wound up in the hospital or run to find a step-by-step way out of the mess.

But not Bernie. He told himself he had simply not yet found the key. His many policies brought him a handsome, steady income but nothing like what he needed. He didn't just want a cash cow; he wanted something big that would bring him respect and dignity and attention, besides a ton of money. He also, as all the motivational tapes and seminars insisted, wanted it to come from something he absolutely loved to do.

He prayed, yes, earnestly and devoutly (albeit ill-advisedly) for something big, really big, to come his way. But the trouble with prayer is that it can be like looking down the barrel of a loaded gun. Too often you get what you ask for. No self-respecting theologian would say God was behind the answer to Bernie's prayer, regardless how persistent he was in it. If there was ever evidence that you can reach just about any goal you devote yourself to, Bernie was it.

For years Bernie Kinney had been nosing around the sports agenting business. He had no contacts, no known abilities, and no knowledge. But he studied. And he sure had an interest. One of the great passions in his life, after money, was sports. All kinds. If he hadn't been a Christian, he said more times than people could count, he'd have probably been a gambler. Of course, he never predicted that he would have gone broke at it, as ninety-nine percent of gamblers do. No, he insisted, he would have made a killing. "I pretend to gamble now, picking winners, you know." He always told people he had picked the champion before the season started. Picked the winner of the title fight. Knew who was going to win the World Series. Yet the claims seemed always to come after the result was known.

But Bernie was not late on his discovery of a mega-talent to represent. After years of having looked into representing athletes, he found a reason. Bernie had uncovered few rules in the agenting game. He didn't have to have a law degree. He didn't even have to register. He would merely speak for a client, that's all. The agreement between him and that client would be their own business.

So, even though he was out of his field and not a lawyer or even a negotiator, Bernie recognized his break when it came. And it came in the form of a sweet, young, naive teenager named Lionel Whalin. The kid was six-foot-ten in the eighth grade. By his senior year of high school he was over seven-feet tall. He had been featured in every mass medium and received a stack of mail from university basketball coaches every day.

Better yet, he was smart and a good kid. He'd been well-raised, was a Christian, and had been a member of First Suburban since childhood. He had been to camp, played on the church softball and basketball teams, and was known to everyone. For years people had snickered about him. Such a string bean. So skinny. A nice boy, though, isn't he? So polite.

Eddie Whalin, Lionel's father, had already had to fend off calls from recruiters, coaches, agents, and advertisers. Bernie Kinney used a subtler approach. He started a couple of years in advance of Lionel's real marketability, cozying up to the Whalin family and talking sports with Eddie. Then, as the time drew near for hard and significant decisions, he had the Whalins out to his house. He let Lionel shoot on his asphalt court with the Plexiglas backboard while he outlined a modest insurance plan for Mr. Whalin that would protect his son against a career-ending injury. Bernie suggested that Lionel's agent share in the cost, because he would stand to lose his percentage of Lionel's income, "should anything untoward happen to the boy, God forbid."

"Agents," Mr. Whalin said. "I've already had my fill of 'em."

Bernie nodded in sympathy. "I'm sure you want someone you know and trust, a Christian who understands Lionel's and your priorities."

"That would be nice. So far all the agents talk about is money."

"I'm sure they see Lionel's unlimited potential," Bernie said.

"I don't know what anybody'd do with millions and millions of dollars anyway," Mr. Whalin said, "and I don't see how anybody's worth that just for playin' a game. It's not his fault he's seven-one and fast as a gazelle."

"But he has worked hard, sir. No one would be interested in him if he was lazy or if he had a bad attitude."

Mr. Whalin appeared pleased that Bernie seemed to know his son so well.

"Forgive me if I'm overstepping," Bernie said.

"No, please."

"Let me just respectfully recommend that you select an agent who would have only your son as a client."

Mr. Whalin looked surprised. "Don't I want someone with lots of experience? And would an agent want to put all his eggs in one basketball player, so to speak?"

"Oh, I'm not sure experience is as necessary as trustworthiness and confidence," Bernie said. "And neither am I suggesting that someone representing your son do that as his only source of income, considerable though it would be. He should perhaps own a business that has built-in services, like phones and clerical help, stationery, and the like."

Mr. Whalin was starting to get the picture. "You wouldn't be interested in the job, would you, Mr. Kinney?"

"Me? Me? Oh, I don't know. I mean, I know sports, and I understand a good bit about the financial end of things. But, oh, you wouldn't want me, would you?"

"I don't know. Maybe not."

"Of course, I do know your family, and there may be ways I could help. I would insist on paying my own expenses."

"Well, maybe you're right. Maybe I should keep thinking about the agents who have been writing and calling."

"I would never accept twenty percent, even if that was standard."

"Oh, Mr. Kinney, if you became Lionel's agent, we would insist on your taking the customary percentage. But—"

"That's very kind of you, but I would want to provide that insurance policy we talked about, or at least a portion of it."

"Well, if we decide to go that way, we can talk about it."

"I'll tell you what, I'll provide that coverage at my own cost, because, as I say, it would also cover me. Now, it's not legal or appropriate for your son to have representation while he's in college, so we'll just have to have a side agreement that commits him to me when he's ready."

"Well—"

"I've taken the liberty of fashioning just such an agreement, which I've had a lawyer review. He agrees that while it is binding, it is also legal and proper."

Bernie produced the papers, and though Mr. Whalin was clearly uneasy, he had no experience in stalling or resisting such an approach. And once the deal was signed, though Bernie Kinney knew full well it violated every collegiate rule for amateur athletes, he was so reassuring and enthusiastic that Eddie Whalin left happy about it. Bernie reminded him to turn away all other forays and to not inform even Lionel about the agreement until he was eligible for the NBA draft.

Later Bernie told his wife, "Lionel's old man is a blue collar worker with a little over-developed sense of conscience, but he's manageable. When he sees what the future holds, he'll look the other way. I love working with simple people."

Bernie's tirelessness paralleled his patience. He had had foresight on the Whalin deal, and he was content to see it play out. He sat on his delicious mystery through Lionel's first two college basketball seasons, and he was gratified to learn that Mr. Whalin was as good a secret keeper as he was. No one knew, and yet everyone suspected. No one could get to the boy, and everyone wanted him.

Lionel had become more than a superstar. He was already a legend. He averaged more than thirty points a game, could handle the ball like a point guard, and could shoot from outside as easily as he could imitate Michael Jordan's monster slam dunks. There was no way this kid would finish college. He would become the highest paid first round draft pick in NBA history.

The only problem was that the better Lionel played, the more Bernie counted on his future. Bernie let his business sag, quit making all those cold calls, refinanced his house, and began looking into investment opportunities. Twenty percent of millions could be a few million itself.

When it was finally time to cash in on Lionel, Bernie needed every dime in a bad way. It was college time for his own kids, and it had been a couple of years since he had turned down any request of his wife. He had an idea, and he studied and prepared how to best pull it off.

His thought was that he would listen to NBA teams and test their interest in his client, but he would ignore the gigantic, multiyear offers. That would be a quick windfall, but not all those years would be guaranteed. Anyway, Bernie's percentage would be only enough to get him out of the hole, not put him on Easy Street. No, the best thing for him, and for his client, would be to take a two-year deal, then hope for a super start by Lionel. If he was everything everyone hoped he would be, his stock would rise and he would then be in line for one of the best deals in professional sports.

By now Lionel was old enough to make his own decisions, and he enjoyed what he heard. Like his parents, his priorities were right. He wasn't in this just for the money, but he also knew it was only good stewardship to expect and accept his proper market value. He was a generous kid, a tither and more, and he had the foresight to handle his own personal finances. Bernie felt bad about that, continually offering to take over that aspect of Lionel's estate too. Lionel may have had some premonition about that, or perhaps Bernie couldn't hide the selfishness in his interest. He would have taken a percentage for that service as well, and he could have taken risks with Lionel's money that he couldn't afford to take with his own. Fortunately for both of them, Lionel retained control.

Representing a basketball star brought more to Bernie than money. It brought him many of the things he sought. He was nearly as much a celebrity at First Church as his client was. Lionel, of course, was seldom there. He lived in the city where he played, and he was in great demand elsewhere. The church was proud of his bold, overt witness for Christ. Short of having him around, they made use of Bernie.

He was invited to speak and often surrounded by young people. They loved to hear him tell of the negotiations and of the other superstars he'd met. They wanted every detail of his meetings with the commissioner of the NBA.

Bernie even developed a humbler, quieter demeanor. He was no longer one who sought out and greeted everyone. Now he waited for them to come to him. And come to him they did. How many parents had asked him to take a look at their son? "He's only second-string in junior high, but he's going to be good. He has such a nice shot in the driveway. If you put in a good word for him somewhere, you'd be his agent. We can promise you that."

Little did they know the odds against two NBA players coming from the same city, let alone the same church. Still, Bernie devoured the attention.

When it first hit the papers that Lionel Whalin's agent had turned down a six-year offer that would have set him up for life in favor of a two-year pact that called for a little more money per season but free agency after that, Bernie was criticized. Sports columnists derided him for gambling with a man's life and career. Sure, they said, Lionel has the confidence and enthusiasm of youth, but the odds are against him. A bad sprain, a broken bone, a head injury, anything could cost him millions.

But Bernie, and Lionel, took the risk. By the end of the first year, they looked like geniuses. By the end of the second, they were dead sure millionaires. Now people had to hand it to Bernie. His gamble had paid off. It may have been risky, even foolhardy. But it was right. Hindsight proved it had been the perfect decision.

Lionel was dominating the game as he had from the opening tip-off of his rookie season. He led the league in scoring and rebounds, led his team to the NBA finals, was a first team all-star, Rookie of the Year, and—despite controversy among purists—named Most Valuable Player. The next season, stunningly, was better. He had become the Wayne Gretzky of basketball. He played with an intensity and maturity never before seen in one so young. He repeated his previous awards, except Rookie of the Year, of course, and this time led his team not just to the finals but also to the championship.

Only time would tell if he would reach Kareem Abdul-Jabbar, Michael Jordan, Julius Erving, Wilt Chamberlain status. But nearly every team in the league wanted to offer him that opportunity. Bernie was ready to strike gold.

He communicated to every interested team that Lionel was looking for a career opportunity. He wanted an eight-year deal, with the money guaranteed, plus a signing bonus equal to twenty percent of the total package. It was bidding time.

One other condition was controversial but not unexpected. The deal had to make Lionel the highest paid player in basketball. That meant a significant raise, but few objected. Sure, there were those who felt that two great years were too few to bank on. But plenty of teams were willing to take the risk.

With other superstars feeling the effects of age, the league and its fans were more than ready for Lionel Whalin. Bernie was lining up endorsement contracts for him that would far outpace his salary. They both knew his performance on the court drove everything else, and the playing contract was his security. Bernie was prepared to milk it for all it was worth.

When it came down to numbers on the table, only the clubs in the two biggest markets, New York and Los Angeles, were still in the running. As the dollars went higher and higher, Bernie was nearly beside himself. He had been featured in major magazines, and the broadcast media had made him a star. But the more the press dug, the more they turned up. Even in the midst of the most exciting and lucrative negotiations in his career, Bernie was exposed as a mediocre insurance salesman at best, an opportunistic friend of the Whalin family at worst. One pundit wondered in print whether it wasn't likely that "Kinney might have had an inappropriate legal relationship with Whalin while Lionel was ostensibly still an amateur."

No one picked up on it except Mr. Whalin. Bernie wouldn't have cared about anyone else. He was in a Los Angeles hotel room on the phone. He sensed New York conceding the deal, but he pleaded with them not to announce they were pulling out. As long as it appeared two teams were still in the running, he could play one off the other. He desperately wanted one more condition, and Los Angeles would never agree unless they were convinced they had to. If New York pulled out and that reached the press, he would have to take L.A.'s last offer. That was no small deal, but it didn't have the killer clause he wanted.

"No," the New York general manager told him, "it's too rich for our blood, and we're going to wish L.A. all the best with the kid. He's been great for basketball. And congratulations to you."

"Thanks. But let me tell you, I'm looking for a no-lower-than clause, and if L.A. won't do it, I may be back to you. So don't announce prematurely."

"A no-lower-than? You mean—"

"A guarantee that Lionel, for the life of the contract, will never be lower than the third highest paid player in the game."

"We already nearly lost our shirts on a deal like that. Anyway, that is pretty sleazy at this stage."

"You can't blame me for trying."

"Yes I can. The public already sees big-time sports as nothing but greed. You just proved it. We're out, and we're saying so."

Bernie quickly switched lines and called the L.A. general manager. He was interrupted by a knock at the door. "Not now! Later!"

"Mr. Kinney, it's Eddie Whalin."

"Just a minute, Eddie!" Bernie quickly got through to L.A. and asked the G.M. to hold. "I want Lionel Whalin's father in here when we agree."

"We've got a deal?"

"Almost."

"What now? Bernie, we've met face to face for hours. Everybody in the country knows it's between us and New York. Now what's it going to take?"

"Your last offer, plus a no-lower-than third clause."

Silence.

"Hello?" Bernie said.

"I'm here, you rat," L.A. said. "You're bringing that into the mix now?"

"It's a deal maker. Do that, and I tell New York it's over."

"And if we don't, it's a deal *breaker?*"

"I didn't say that."

"I'll have to call you back."

"No! No! I'll hold, but I gotta know." Eddie knocked again. Bernie covered the phone. "Just a minute, Eddie, please!" Back to the G.M. "I gotta know now."

There was a long pause. "What you're tellin' me, Kinney, is that New York turned you down on this, but you still want it from us. If we say no, are we still in it?"

Bernie grimaced and tried not to look deep within himself. There wouldn't have been far to look. He quickly told himself he had to keep the best interests of his client in mind. He could shade the truth without lying, couldn't he?

Knock! Knock!

"Just a minute, Eddie!"

"Well, Bernie?"

"Without the no-lower-than clause, you've got a good chance of losing the deal."

A huge sigh. "All right. Hang on."

Bernie jumped up and let Eddie in. "Eddie, good to see you, man. I'm on the final call right now. Look at these numbers." He showed Mr. Whalin the number of years, the amount of dollars, the 20 percent signing bonus, and the no-lower-than clause. Eddie did not change expression.

"I need to know, Bernie, if the agreement you and I had before Lionel turned pro was ethical."

Bernie picked up the phone to listen and covered the mouthpiece. "'Course. 'Course it was, I told you."

"I know what you told me. It may have been legal, but it was wrong ethically, according to the NCAA, wasn't it?"

"Oh, it may have stretched a rule, but no harm was done, huh? We're not talking about laws here. We're talking about guidelines, in-house rules. Everybody stretches 'em. It's part of the game."

"We're talking about cheating and lying, Bernie. Lying to me."

"Eddie!" Bernie turned back to the phone. "Yeah! OK? We got a deal? Everything we talked about? Great! You won't be sorry! I'll have the papers delivered!"

Bernie could barely contain himself. He tried to embrace Mr. Whalin. "We did it! The biggest deal in history!"

"You cheated, Bernie. You call yourself a brother, and you cheated. I have to call Lionel now."

"So do I. Let me tell him, would you? I know he's waiting by the phone."

"You can tell him about the deal, Bernie, but I have to tell him what you did. I don't know what he's gonna do about it."

"How can he be mad when I've just made him the richest team athlete in history?"

Bernie dialed. In the midst of the conversation, he made a suggestion to Lionel. "You could just pass the signing bonus on to me. It works out to exactly what my commission would be over the next eight years. Then you wouldn't have to worry about my cut of salary dollars after that. . . . Well, sure, we can discuss that later. Listen, your dad wants to talk to you. Yeah! He's right here! I think he's happy, sure!"

But, of course, he wasn't.

To Lionel's credit, he was a trusting soul. Though he felt obligated as a Christian to bring the facts to light, he also believed Bernie's excuses. Bernie would make it right. Lionel was even naive enough to advance Bernie some of his commission to pay the heavy fine for his indiscretion.

Taffy Kinney would not let up on her husband. She worried more about the reduction in family income than about her husband's morals.

"How did you think you could get away with it?" she said.

"That's just it, hon," he said. "I did get away with it. Eddie Whalin and Lionel are so solidly in my corner now that I've bought lifetime security."

"Nothing else they can get you on?"

"Not a thing."

But greed knows no bounds. When Bernie got used to his windfall and stretched his credit to its new limits, he tried another scheme, again without his client's knowledge. Only this time he tried it with the wrong man.

Bernie had waited eighteen months until two players surpassed Lionel in annual income, then he approached the general manager of the club most likely to next increase the pay of a superstar. The idea was simple, as Bernie explained it to the G.M. on a long, private walk in the woods. "You be as generous as you can without drawing suspicion. You make your guy third highest-paid player in the NBA. That makes my guy fourth and forces L.A. to increase him. You and I split my commission. The more generous you are, the more you get. We both know it'll be more than you'll make in years at your job."

The G.M. bit. Or at least Bernie thought he had. But there are still honest men in some pockets of big-time sports, and Bernie had chosen one who wanted to see the game and the business remain ethical, even as its dollars spiraled crazily. With the help of the FBI and the cooperation of the player, Bernie was stung and stung hard. When he passed along the G.M.'s cut, he was arrested.

Most painful for Bernie was a question from his former client. "Mr. Kinney," Lionel asked, "how will people judge our church now? By you or by me?"

"More important," Eddie Whalin said, "how will they judge the Lord? I would not want that on my conscience, Bernie. Huh-uh."

The blue collar worker and his formerly naive son had stood for what was right and eventually rose above the stain of their unscrupulous agent. Bernie Kinney went to jail.

THE SPURIOUS PARAMOUR

Roger Rhodes had a problem he could share with no one. As head of counseling at First Suburban Church, he was obligated to confidentiality. By policy he didn't even share things with the pastor without a counselee's permission—especially if that counselee was also a staff member.

Roger was mainly a marriage counselor. He delegated much of the other work. These days there were more marital problems than ever. Not only had one of the pastor's favorite employees come to Roger with a serious problem, but the young man's wife wanted to see him now—without her husband's knowledge.

After talking with the young husband several months before, he had been encouraged. What, then, did the wife want?

Pastor Nigel Ingle had been so distressed about the state of marriage in the nineties that he asked Roger to hold a mini-seminar for the leaders of the church. "Our colleagues across the country are dropping like flies," Nigel told him. "Woe to us if we stand by and watch it happen here."

Roger's seminar stressed building better communication, fostering mutual respect, renewing romance, and practicing healthier finances—cures for the most common causes of marital discord. But a few months later, youth pastor Jason Dozier, a star of the staff, had come to him with a delicate problem. The church's thirty-year-old youth man had always been a free-lancer. He was wonderful-looking, a dark, handsome, tall man with a gorgeous wife, a beautiful singing voice, talent on the guitar, and a personality that endeared him to people of all ages. The surprising thing about Jason was that he had enough personality that he seemed to turn off no one. Too often a young person with that much going for him evidenced at least enough pride to generate some resentment. Not Jason. He was a truly humble, spiritual guy, "in the Word," as they say about someone who studies his Bible every day. The kids, especially the girls, adored him. Their parents shared that enthusiasm. He kept in touch with people, followed through on commitments, was careful about his private life (deftly and affirmingly deflecting adolescent—and not-so-adolescent—crushes), and was also a good speaker and teacher.

Roger knew that Nigel Ingle was duly proud of Jason. He had handpicked him and trained and discipled him, mentored him, and had seen him blossom. Nigel counseled Jason on how to field speaking and teaching requests, and he sold the board on allowing Jason to make a little money on the side as a consultant.

With everything else in his life apparently under control and going swimmingly, Jason quietly told Roger that he had found himself sexually impotent. "Annie has been patient and sympathetic, but of course I don't want sympathy. She's almost two years older than I am and wants a family." Needless to say, he wanted to find a solution quickly.

Roger interviewed Jason at length and suggested that he was overworked, stressed, and under-rested. "I would counsel you to cut back on your moonlighting, and I want you to see a physician just to be sure there's nothing physically wrong. Meanwhile, let me see what I can do about your work load."

"I'm not complaining about my ministry," Jason said.

"I know, but it's a staff-wide problem."

"Not to be disrespectful, Mr. Rhodes, but what can you do about it? I mean, you don't set the hours."

"Oh, I think the pastor will listen to me if I see too many people putting in too many hours at the expense of their marriages and families."

"But you don't have to tell him about—"

"Of course not."

Later, Roger told the pastor, "The seminar was your idea. And it was a good one. But one of my main themes either fell on deaf ears or came from the wrong source."

"Which one?"

"The one about carving out time and spending more hours with each other." Roger felt awkward about not telling the most stark reason for his meeting with the pastor, but he could not.

"Oh, Roger," Nigel said, "I think people heard you and appreciated that one. I did. And though Jen and I were doing well in that area, we're doing even better now. Be encouraged."

Roger smiled. "You stepped right into my trap."

"Uh-oh."

"Pastor, your leadership staff heard me too, but they didn't hear you."

"They know how I feel about this, Rog. I support it. I support you. I model it."

"You model it, but you don't give your staff the freedom to follow your example."

"I'll bite. What are you saying?"

"I'm saying that people can listen to me, and they can know what's right, but until their boss actually gives them permission to change their priorities, they never will."

"Roger, you know I don't—"

"Like to see yourself as a boss, I know. But let's face it. People defer to you. They work for you—for the Lord, ultimately, of course, but for you, humanly speaking. What I'm looking for is a directive."

"You want me to force them to spend more time with their spouses?"

"You can't force them. But you *can* take away their alibis. Many on your staff are so immersed in ministry that they're giving their marriages leftover time. Or they're into quality time, which we both know—"

"Is a myth."

"Precisely."

"But we have a lot of hurting people in our congregation, Rog. People who need help and attention."

"Yet I've heard you say that if we minister to everyone else and lose our own marriages and families, we've lost in the end."

"You're not going to let me up, are you, Roger?"

"Hey, I report to you, too. I'm just advising, pleading the case for a directive that sets guidelines."

"But what if they use the extra time away from the church just playing and still ignore their spouses?"

"That's their problem. We can't force them to do the right thing, but like like I said, we can keep from being the reason they do the wrong thing."

128

The pastor leaned back in his chair and studied his chief counselor. "You've got it," he said.

"I've got it? You don't even want to think about it for a few days?"

"Quit while you're ahead, Rog. You've got me so inspired to spend more time with my wife, I won't have time to think about it."

"What'll the policy be, Pastor?"

"What do you recommend?"

"That no staffer should work more than ten hours a day, no more than five days a week, and that includes no more than two evenings a week."

"Ouch. Anything else?"

"I think you should require, or at least strongly urge, that those two nights be negotiated in advance with the spouse."

"I like it."

"One more thing."

"Only one?"

"I promise. Once you've made the directive, tell the congregation. That way they'll understand when there isn't someone available twenty-four hours a day."

"There will be exceptions, though, Rog. There are times when we all have to flex."

"Of course."

The directive and the announcement were met with enthusiasm by both the staff and the congregation. The staff at First Church had developed a reputation as anything but slackers. Apparently the congregation agreed that they deserved more sensible hours and more reasonable demands on their time.

Jason Dozier did not ask for a follow-up appointment, so Roger had to seek him out. "Everything OK at home?"

Jason merely smiled, gave a thumbs-up sign, and whispered, "It was physical, and it's been taken care of."

Roger had a nagging feeling that the solution had been too easy, and he wished he could have pointed to the new staff freedom (if that's what you call "cutting back" to a fifty-hour work week) as at least part of the cure. With the new edict from the pastor, a staffer such as Jason found himself with two full weekdays off. As many of his youth activities took place on Saturday and Sunday, and many more occurred in the evenings, he frequently put in four ten-hour days that began at noon (including Saturday), and he easily logged ten hours on Sundays.

No one had the impression that Jason was giving less than his best to the ministry to which he had been called, nominated, voted into, and paid for. Some of the kids complained that he was no longer available on Mondays and Tuesdays, or Wednesday through Friday mornings, but when school started, no one noticed much. Except, perhaps, his beauteous wife.

When Annie Dozier called for an appointment, Roger, not wanting to enmesh himself in a complicated, double-confidential situation, tried to avoid it. "By policy, I can't," he explained. "Sue usually handles the women."

"This is marital."

"Oh, well, then, um, I'd be more than happy to meet with both of you."

"He can't know I'm talking to you yet."

"I see. Annie, help me out. How serious a problem do we have?"

She paused. "Let's just say it needs immediate attention."

"Please don't read anything into this, but I need to know. Is there a moral problem?"

There was a longer pause. "If you're talking sexual infidelity, I don't know." Despite his training, Roger had never fully gotten used to the younger generation speaking so openly. Even the possibility of a moral problem with Jason Dozier made his heart sink.

"Annie, you understand why I can't meet with you alone. Do you hope or expect that eventually Jason will be brought into these discussions?"

"Yes."

"Then I think I'd better find a third party."

"How about the pastor?"

Roger winced. "That might appear to be ganging up."

"We might *be* ganging up."

"Think about this, Annie. I'd like to bring in an older, more mature woman. It's biblical to have older women counseling the younger."

"But not counseling young men."

"I'll handle that part of it when the time comes. Or I'll assign someone."

"Who did you have in mind for our meeting?" Annie said.

"Bernice Pinder."

Annie laughed. "I'm sorry," she said, "but I was so certain you were going to say *Evelyn* Pinder that I can hardly believe you said her mother. She must be, what—?"

"Seventy-four and as feisty an old gal as you'll meet. You want to meet with her alone?"

"No. I do want someone on staff to know what's going on."

Bernice Pinder accepted her assignment with relish. Tall and rail-thin, she showed up with her heavily-marked Bible, her full head of snow-white hair, and a Southern accent uncompromised by thirty years of life in the North. "I'm a widdah," she said, meaning widow, "but Waltah and I had neahly forty-six yeahs togethah. You cain't shock me."

Annie Dozier was a stark contrast. Her straight black hair was cut evenly at the shoulders, and she was petite and striking.

"I don't want to shock anyone," Annie said. "I'm just worried about Jason."

She told the story of how disciplined Jason was and always had been. "I'm surprised at how good a counselor he is, because he really shouldn't have much patience with people unwilling to work at their problems. Most people want things to come easy. He works at everything. He sets a schedule and keeps it, stays in shape, gets up on time, goes to bed on time, eats right, prepares, studies, and has always seemed truly spiritual."

"I can see why you've come for help," Mrs. Pinder teased, laughing aloud at herself.

"I know what you mean," Annie said. "I should probably be ashamed of myself. Up till the last five months or so, I believed I was married to the perfect man. You both know how much people love him."

"We do," Roger agreed.

"He has a ministry," Annie said. "And time for everything else. His outside consulting hours had been limited by the time he had to be at church."

Roger almost blurted that he had advised Jason to drop the outside work. Of course he couldn't betray that confidence, but still it troubled him that Jason apparently ignored the advice without arguing the point.

"As soon as Pastor Ingle came out with that new policy, Jason started advertising," Annie said. "He had stationery printed and sent out letters to a huge mailing list of churches and businesses, offering his services as a computer analyst and management consultant."

"Computers and management?" Roger said.

Annie nodded. "Surprised?"

"I am!" Mrs. Pinder said. "Like that boy needs more strengths!"

"People who think they know him don't realize that he really is a sort of a Renaissance man," Annie said. "Everyone knows he's a consultant to other ministries, but besides all the stuff at church he does so well, he's also enough of an expert in management and computers that he makes a lot of money at it on the side."

Somehow those abilities had never come to light at First Church. There had been a good bit of management advice in a paperback book he had written for a Sunday school publishing house, but in the main it was a youth worker's and assistant pastor's manual, so few noticed. The consulting Jason had done in the past was for other churches in the areas in which he worked at First Church. He had made a little money at it, but now that he had more free time, apparently he had opened a consulting business. The approval had come in advance. He was merely doing more of what he had been doing.

"Anyway," Annie continued, "he built himself a business in the den of our home, and he has everything there. He's rented a fax machine, a computer with a modem, a copy machine, and an answering machine. If you need it to run a business, he's got it."

Mrs. Pinder looked impressed. "Wonder why he's only rented the stuff," she said. "Is this temporary?'

"He may want me to think it is, but it sure takes a lot of his time."

Roger Rhodes was troubled, his chin propped up by his hand. "When does he do all this, Annie?"

"Every spare moment."

"Be specific."

She sighed, then took a deep breath, thinking. "He gets up at five, studies his Bible for half an hour, then runs for another half hour. He showers and eats by six-thirty, then starts making his calls to the East Coast."

"The East Coast?" Mrs. Pinder said.

"Because of the time difference."

"I understand that," she drawled. "But what business does he have way out there?"

"Mrs. Pinder, he has business all over the country."

"Continue with his schedule," Roger said.

"Well, Mondays and Tuesdays he's either in his den or out with clients all day and all evening."

"What do you mean by all evening?"

"Till nine or ten."

"My, my," the older woman said.

"So you never see him."

"Well, he's pretty good about lunch and dinner with me, when he's home, but he's rarely home. We'll go out or he'll eat with me at home, but it's only half an hour, and then he's back at it."

"I don't get this," Mrs. Pinder said. "What is he back at?"

"His consulting business. He advises managers on computer systems and even personnel matters. He also handles all his speaking engagements and concerts from the business."

"But you do get time with him."

"At meal times when he's home."

"What about the rest of the week?" Roger said. "Does he sleep in in the mornings? I know he gets in here right after lunch most days, because of the late nights and the busyness of the weekends."

Annie chuckled. "He doesn't know the meaning of the words *sleep in.* When his head hits the pillow at eleven, he's out, and he's in such good shape that the six hours he gets every night is plenty."

"Forgive me for bein' so bold," Mrs. Pinder said, "but how's your love life?"

Roger watched Annie carefully. She looked down. "We had a few problems some time ago, but I can't complain now."

Roger was relieved, and glad to change the subject. "So he works in his den on weekday mornings too?"

She nodded. "Wednesday through Friday."

"After all day Monday and Tuesday."

Annie seemed to be finished, but Roger knew there was more. "Let me tell you what I'm hearing," he tried. "You're married to a wonderful, dedicated, committed, disciplined, accomplished man that most women would die for."

She nodded again.

"But you suspect him."

"He said we could start a family when his job as youth pastor settled down. We used to kid about the fact that it probably never would. For a couple of years he even talked about getting out of youth work, staying with the pastorate but moving into some other area."

"I remember him talking about that to the pastor," Roger said. "Nigel wanted him to replace himself first, and then, when the new work policy came down, Jason quit talking about it."

"And see," Annie said, "I was glad about that. For years Jason has talked about people wanting to get out of youth work, as if moving to something else is a step up or as if youth work is just a stepping stone to something else. Everybody knows the statistics about how quickly youth men move on."

"I don't," Mrs. Pinder said. "Guess we've been spoiled."

"Well, Jason's been here since he graduated from college, full-time for almost eight years."

"And most others leave how soon?" Mrs. Pinder said.

"I've heard something like eighteen months," Annie said. Roger nodded. Mrs. Pinder shook her head. "I know Jason could be a senior pastor some day," Annie continued, "but I don't think he's called to that or wants that. He loves the kids and his ministry with them and would stay as long as he was wanted here."

"You can rest assured that unless he's somehow disqualified himself, he'll be here as long as Nigel Ingle is here," Roger predicted.

"I know, but don't you see? Jason's job did settle down. It became sensible and workable. I didn't expect any more long walks on the beach or days filled with small talk. That's not Jason, and I wouldn't force him into that."

"Is it *you?*" Mrs. Pinder asked. "Because it sounds like you're remarkably flexible with him. If you want long walks and small talk once in a while, maybe there could be some tradeoffs."

"I have nothing to trade, and anyway, I couldn't complain. How could I criticize a husband who did everything so perfectly?"

"Don't ask me," Mrs. Pinder roared. "That certainly wasn't Walter! But then, we were a lot alike. I daresay you and your husband are more similar that you think."

Annie didn't respond. "Most people don't know that I'm almost two years older than Jason."

"You could have fooled me," Mrs. Pinder said.

"Thanks. But you can see why I would like him to make good on his promise. He doesn't have to work seven, or even six days a week anymore. I agreed that would be no schedule for a new father, but now—"

"Well," the old woman said, "what does he say?"

With that, Annie's reserves were exhausted and she broke down. Mrs. Pinder put a hand on her shoulder as she sobbed. Roger waited. "He doesn't seem to want to talk about having children at all."

"A man like that, with that much to offer?" Mrs. Pinder said. "And a wife who wants to be a mother?"

"He usually just changes the subject."

"Thinks kids would get in the way of his career?" Mrs. Pinder said.

"I don't know! I can't imagine he'd feel that way."

"I need to talk to him," Mrs. Pinder said. "I just hope he doesn't think he's too important to the kingdom or the world or whatever to be bothered with being a father."

That charge Annie Dozier did not deny, but Roger knew that something else was on her mind. "Annie," he said carefully, "we care and we love you both, and we want to help. Why do you suspect him?"

Annie lost control again, then dug from her purse a photo copy of a handwritten note. "I know this is going to come as a shock to you, Mr. Rhodes," she said, "but he's averaging more a month in outside work than he makes at the church, at least for the last five months."

Shock was an understatement. Roger was nearly speechless. "Annie," he managed, "what is he doing with the money?"

"Mostly he's been wise and frugal. Lots of sound investments. But I worry too."

"About?"

"About this," she said, thrusting out the note.

Roger read it and lowered his head, then looked at Annie for permission to show it to Mrs. Pinder. Annie nodded and wept. Mrs. Pinder looked at the note, carefully folded it, and handed it back to Annie. "Where did you get this?" she asked.

"I snooped. I know that's terrible, but I had to know what what was going on. He has that second phone line for the fax machine and his business, and I know he spends a lot of time on it. The desk and the file cabinets are always locked, but I found his appointment book. There were a lot of notations in there about appointments with Dolly, and that note was paper-clipped to one page."

It read:

Dear Dolly, you've made me the happiest man alive. I agree I should be telling Annie soon. Call you later. Love, Jason.

"I don't want to overreact," Roger said. "But it sounds like early mid-life crisis."

"Psycho-babble!" Mrs. Pinder said. "It's time for a confrontation."

"I wonder if Jason has yuppie disease."

"Now there's a term out of the eighties!" Mrs. Pinder said. "Even I know what a yuppie is. A young, upwardly mobile professional."

Annie pursed her lips and nodded. "Only we're becoming dinks."

"That's a new one on me," Mrs. Pinder said. "But I'm ready. What's it stand for?"

"Double income, no kids. He wanted me to work too. I'm just afraid the only reason he doesn't want children is because it would slow down his income."

"That doesn't sound like him," Roger said.

"Neither does that note," Mrs. Pinder said. "But there it is."

"Annie," Roger said carefully, "tell me what you're feeling."

She took a fluttery breath. "Betrayed. Foolish. Desperate."

"Shall I call him now and get him over here?"

"I get to be in on that one too, don't I, Mr. Rhodes?" Mrs. Pinder said.

"That's up to Annie."

The young wife nodded miserably. "I'd appreciate it. But don't be too hard on him."

"No promises," Mrs. Pinder said.

"Where is he?" Roger said.

"I believe he's finishing up at Village Church this morning. Some computer system."

Roger dialed and the pastor answered. "Dale!" he said. "Roger Rhodes. Fine. Listen, is Jason Dozier over there? Oh, he did? Thanks."

He hung up and dialed again. "Finished early. Said he was going home."

"I'll bet," Annie said.

Roger turned back to the phone. "Uh, hello. Who's this? Yeah. Would you tell him that Roger Rhodes called and would like to see him as soon as possible at the church. . . . Has he? Well, Miss Crawford, if you had the time, maybe you'd come with him. Oh, Mrs. Crawford, excuse me. Yes, see you soon."

Annie's eyes widened. "That was—?"

"Dolly Crawford."

"At my house?!"

"She said Mr. Dozier was on the other phone and asked her to answer that one. You're about to meet her."

"I'm not sure I'm ready for that. She said she was married?"

Roger nodded. "Also said Jason had told her a lot about me."

Jason was stunned to find his weepy wife with Roger and Mrs. Pinder, but no more shocked than they were to get their first glimpse of Dolly Crawford. She was a matronly, sixtyish woman, stocky and pleasant with a huge smile. She appeared to want to embrace Annie, but the young woman did not make herself available.

"Annie," Jason whispered as he sat, "did you use the copy machine?"

She nodded.

"You left it on."

"Sorry. Guess I was more concerned with returning the original of this to your date book."

He looked at the note, laughed, and showed it to Dolly. "I told you this was dangerous way to go, Mr. Dozier," she said, smiling. "The jig is up. It's time to explain."

"Well, I hadn't expected to have to tell personal things with an audience."

"I'll leave," Mrs. Pinder said.

"So will I," Roger said. "But I confess I'm curious."

"No, please stay. I can only imagine what you must think. Roger, when I went to the physician about the other problem we discussed—forgive me for not going into detail—he had a quick solution. He could not, however, do anything about my sterility."

Annie gasped.

"I didn't want to tell you, hon, until I was sure and until I had exhausted all avenues. I knew how much you wanted a baby. I didn't even want you to know about my meetings with Mrs. Crawford, because there's such a long a wait, and sometimes hopes get dashed."

"Hopes for what?"

Mrs. Crawford leaned forward and thrust out a strong hand. "We have not been properly introduced, Annie. I'm Dolly Crawford of the Family Services Agency. Your husband here has been hoarding money for months in case we had to go international for your baby. We have a young pregnant girl in New York and one right here in town and also just received pictures of some young orphans from both the Philippines and South America, if you want to go that route."

"I had expected to find you at home," Jason said, "because I thought it was time you met the woman who's going to find us a child. I'm sorry to have been so mysterious. I wanted it to be a wonderful surprise, not something that caused you pain."

"I'll get over it," she said, tears of relief on her face as she leaned to embrace him. "Now let me see the pictures!"

TRUTH
AND TIME

It's a rare and ugly thing when a church is surrounded by flashing emergency lights in the night. They usually indicate a fire in the bowels of the place or that someone has suffered a cardiac arrest.

Or worse.

One evening at First Suburban, a few weeks before the advent of spring, it was worse. Someone had been murdered.

The someone was Thomas Noel, a forty-one-year-old father of two grown daughters and a regular attender of the church for thirty-five years. He had breathed his last in the arms of an elderly woman on the floor of the men's washroom off the main foyer. Ironically it was Dorcas Ivins, Mr. Noel's first Sunday school teacher, who had cradled the bleeding, rasping man as he fought for air. She alternately screamed for help and tried to

soothe him—telling him he would be all right. He hadn't needed her cries to convince him of the seriousness of his situation.
A pair of tiny manicuring scissors had both punctured a lung
and severed his carotid artery. He might have survived the
wound to his chest, but the laceration in his neck caused life to
flow from him in a red pool.

Most bizarre was that the widow Ivins insisted she had
done the deed.

With the senior pastor out of town and most of the ministries over for the night, counseling pastor Roger Rhodes was
responsible for locking up. He had had a couple of late ses-
sions, as had one of his assistants, Sue Runnels. By policy she
had left the building with her last counselee. Roger had heard
the choir file out about twenty minutes before he finished with
his last appointment. A teachers' meeting downstairs had gone
long, and he had considered making a brief appearance to urge
a timely end so he could close up and head home. When he
heard activity in the foyer he assumed the meeting had broken
up.

He was wrong. Something was amiss, but it didn't pene-
trate his consciousness until he heard the screaming. No one
should have been in the foyer. First Suburban is one of those
churches where the front door is used only on Sundays when
crowds pour in and where new people use it as the logical en-
trance. On a night of meetings, the crowd is made up of veter-
ans who know the most convenient entrances. They come in
directly from the parking lot in the back. The front is dark, and
the door is locked.

Pastor Rhodes had noticed nothing else out of the ordinary
as he shut his door and heard the faint cries from the other end
of the hall. His first thought was that it sounded like the gym on
children's club night. But as he moved toward the intermittent
sound he realized it was an adult voice, pleading—a woman,

desperate and terrified. Roger hurried but didn't break into a run. His mind was filled with images of horror. Would he come upon a rape, a bad accident, a robbery, what? He wanted to hear what she was screaming about before he got there.

"Help me! Oh, please, somebody help me! He's dying!"

And then Roger ran.

He followed the sounds to the mostly dark foyer but couldn't place their origin any more specifically. Lights shone under the doors of both washrooms. He knocked quickly at the women's, but before he pushed, the woman screamed again and he knew she was in the men's.

Roger chastised himself for his instinct to knock before entering. The woman was shrieking now, sobbing, moaning. "He's dying! He's dying! Help me!"

Roger flung open the door and saw Mrs. Ivins cradling the torso of a clearly lifeless man. "It's Tommy, Pastor!" she wailed. "It's Tommy!"

"What happened?" he said as he hurried to the man and felt for a pulse, recognizing him as Tom Noel. Detecting no heartbeat, Roger gently laid the man on the floor and helped the wobbly woman to her feet. She trembled, and he dismissed his idea of asking her to call the paramedics and police. He handed her his keys and asked if she was collected enough to let herself into his office and wait for him there.

"He's dead, isn't he, Pastor?" she said.

He rose and embraced her as she sobbed. "I'm afraid he is, dear. Do you know what happened?" She shook her head. "Can you wait in my office?" She nodded.

Roger shuddered as he turned back to the unseeing eyes of Thomas Noel. He draped his own overcoat over the body, noticing that Tom's blood seemed to have come from the neck. Roger didn't notice the second source of blood, for it had all run together.

Not far from the body was a cheap, gold-painted pair of manicure scissors, similar to the ones found in personal hygiene kits given away as promotional gimmicks. Roger squinted, thinking. He had seen something similar recently. Where? At home? He reached for them, then froze as he heard someone else scream and run toward the washroom. Roger realized he would have been a fool to have handled what appeared to be the murder weapon. Now he had to keep others from the room.

"Please stay out!" he hollered as the footsteps neared the door. The door swung partially open.

"Mrs. Ivins says someone is dead in here," a familiar female voice said.

It was Mrs. Grom, who had apparently come upon the blood-caked Dorcas Ivins in the hall. "Oh, Marjorie, please don't come in," Roger said. "We do need the paramedics and the police. Could you call?"

During the interminable minutes before the lights began flashing outside the building, Roger stationed himself before the washroom door. He asked Marjorie to sit with Dorcas in his office, and he asked everyone else to please leave. No, he couldn't let anyone in. No, he didn't know exactly what had happened. No, he didn't want to say who the victim was.

No one left. They all waited for a glimpse. And it wasn't long before the news spread from Roger's office, where Dorcas Ivins wept with Marjorie Grom, who the dead man was.

"Is it really Tom Noel?"

Roger didn't want to say, but his look gave him away.

"Please don't let this news get to his family before they're properly informed," he begged. "Is the choir gone?" Someone said they were, and he heaved a sigh. Both Mrs. Noel and her older daughter had been at choir practice. He was so grateful they had not been here to see this. But people ignored his plea to keep it quiet. They were soon calling their own families, and more and more began to arrive.

An hour later the coroner pronounced Tom dead, and his body was wheeled out. The police had secured the church and dismissed all those they determined had recently arrived. Forensics personnel shot pictures and examined foyer, hallway, and washroom, and uniformed officers began questioning people.

A plainclothes detective looked impassively at the blood-stained washroom door and a plastic bag containing the scissors, then singled out Roger. He introduced himself as homicide sergeant Hollis Grew and walked Roger to his office. As they approached the door, Marjorie Grom stepped out. She looked at Detective Grew and asked if he minded if she had a second with Pastor Rhodes.

Out of earshot of the sergeant, she whispered, "You're not going to believe this, but Dorcas wants to confess."

Marjorie was right; Roger couldn't believe it. If there was a saint at First Suburban, it was Dorcas Ivins. She had been teaching Sunday school for more than forty-nine years, and anyone there since childhood had had her as a teacher. No way did this fit her character. Roger decided to go on the offensive with Grew.

"I need to tell you something before you talk to the woman who found the victim," he said. Grew pursed his lips and stared as if to say he was listening but not agreeing to anything in advance. "She's trying to say she did it, but listen, she's—"

Grew help up a hand. "You found her with the dead guy in her arms, and now she wants to confess? She's gonna make my work easier and my night shorter."

"But I'm telling you—"

"No! I'm telling you, if you want to sit in with us, which I'd like the other lady to do as well, or if you'd like to advise her to

147

get a lawyer—which I will also do, feel free. But don't be telling me anything until I've talked to her."

Suitably chastised, Roger followed the detective into his own office. Dorcas Ivins looked as if she'd been in a war. Her hands and her neck and her bulky winter coat were blood-caked. She sat staring, as if in a trance. Marjorie Grom fluttered about until Hollis Grew steadied her with a perturbed gaze, and she sat with the others.

The otherwise impatient Detective Grew waxed tender as he sat knee-to-knee with Mrs. Ivins. He gently took one of her hands in his and leaned close. "Can you hear and understand me, ma'am?"

She nodded.

Grew peeked at his notes. "You name is Dorcas Ivins?"

She nodded again.

"Please respond orally, ma'am."

"Yes, I'm Dorcas Ivins." And she gave her address.

"Mrs. Ivins, you're under arrest for the murder of Thomas Noel. You have the right to remain silent. Anything you say—"

"You're arresting her?" Roger blurted, but he fell silent under a hard glare from Grew.

"Anything you say can and will be used against you in a court of law. You have the right to an attorney. If you cannot afford one, one will be provided for you. Do you understand these rights as I have explained them to you?"

Mrs. Ivins nodded, then quickly added, "Yes."

"Do you wish to waive your rights to silence or to an attorney?"

"Yes."

"We have a a good lawyer in our church, Dorcas," Roger interrupted.

Hollis Grew wheeled in his chair to face the counseling

pastor. "She has waived her right to an attorney, sir. If you'd rather wait outside—"

"She's also a distraught, elderly woman who saw a man die," Rhodes said, trying to keep from raising his voice.

"It's all right, Roger," Mrs. Ivins thin voice assured him. "I don't mind telling why I did it."

The three witnesses in Roger's office heard a weird story that night.

"I was at the Sunday school teachers' meeting," she began. "They think I don't know they've got a fiftieth anniversary bash planned for me next month. They ought to figure I wasn't born yesterday. Well, I guess that party will never happen." She stopped and shook her head, gazing wistfully at nothing in the distance.

"Anyway, we were covering all the usual stuff, these kids in their forties and fifties pretending to know everything about children and what they need to learn. What they need, Roger, as you know, is someone to love them, someone to convince them they're special." She hesitated again, as if picking up steam. She intoned the following as if it were her own dictum, and Roger couldn't be sure it wasn't: "Every child needs one person to think he's the most important person in the world."

Mrs. Ivins's lips trembled and she looked down, seeming to notice the blood for the first time. "I don't want the blood of any children on my hands," she whispered. "Not even Tommy's, though he disappointed me so."

"How did he disappoint you, ma'am?" Hollis Grew asked gently.

"I never would have suspected anything of him," she said. "Not Tommy. But there was no mistaking it."

"No mistaking what, ma'am?"

"Women troubles," she said. "That's what it always is today. Women."

"Could you start at the beginning, Mrs. Ivins?"

"Couldn't you let her get cleaned up a little first?" Roger pleaded.

Grew held up a hand for silence without looking at Roger.

"Well, our meeting was going late," the old woman continued, "and as it does too often nowadays, nature called." She looked up, suddenly self-conscious. "Excuse me," she said. Roger thought it ironic that she was confessing to a murder and embarrassed to speak of personal necessities.

"The ladies' room in the basement gives me the willies, so I excused myself and came up to the one off the foyer. I figured the meeting would be over by the time I got back, so I took all my stuff with me so they'd know I was leaving. Nobody cares about that anymore. It's one of the privileges of being an old lady." She smiled, but no one else did. Roger had a sinking feeling. He had always noticed a certain sincerity in her voice, a quality he had hoped would be absent just now. She sounded genuine. Would she, could she convince him she had murdered a husky man in the prime of his life?

Roger's heart began to race when he realized why the manicuring scissors had seemed so familiar. His wife had received a cheap kit with the "gold" cuticle remover, scissors, nail file, and the like with her mail order purchase of something or other. It was a gaudy gift with a fake patent leather case for the garish utensils. She had given it to their six-year-old daughter, reminding her to be careful.

Suzie had brought that case and those chintzy tools into his office that very morning. They had quarreled about them because he didn't want her to take them to school and had recalled his wife telling her the same. Had he touched those scissors? Yes, he recalled. He had taken them from her, returned them to the case, and dropped the case in his bottom desk drawer, where they were now.

Roger began to feel like a character in an Edgar Allan Poe story. Evidence linking him to the murder weapon was within inches of the detective's nose as he sat interviewing a most unlikely suspect. Beyond all reason, Roger was compelled to check for himself right then.

As Mrs. Ivins continued her elaborate story, Roger leaned past Detective Grew to open his desk drawer. With his body shielding everyone else's view, he peered into the catch-all drawer and saw the patent leather case, lying open, the scissors missing from their sleeve. With as much calm as he could muster he slid the drawer shut and sat back.

One thing Roger knew for sure: he had not opened that drawer since dropping the case in there. Now the questions were: If those scissors were the murder weapon, would they have his fingerprints on them? His fingerprints would surely be on the men's room door. More important, who had access to the scissors and would have murdered Tom Noel with them?

Mrs. Ivins had launched into her story about overhearing a conversation between Tom and his wife in the foyer while she was still in the ladies' room. That made sense. Choir practice had broken up. Had anyone in the choir seen Mrs. Noel head toward the foyer rather than out the back, the way everyone else left? No doubt Hollis Grew and his people would find out soon enough. And what about the Noel daughter, Parke? Had she been at choir practice too? Had she come with her mother? Had they left together? Had she seen her father as well? What had he been doing at the church? He usually worked nights.

Tom Noel was one great guy. A servant. You could always count on him to be there for work days. He was the one who would carry things, paint, clean, do anything. A lot of people showed up for those projects and created a lot of dust for half an hour, but then they knew how to look busy or disappear or be in charge of refreshments or running errands. Tom was the one who would put in hours of sweat and would be whipped by the end of the day.

He was not a leader or a teacher or an overtly spiritual guy. Solid. That was how you would describe him. He was known as a quietly proud family man. Who would want to kill him?

Now Mrs. Ivins, the saint of all saints at First Church, claimed she had gone from a half-century of selfless service in Sunday school to a murderous rage in the space of a minute or two of overhearing a conversation between a man and his wife. Hollis Grew wanted to know the gist of what she had heard. It was clear to Roger that Grew was becoming as skeptical as he.

"She said she had mistakenly opened a letter addressed to him and that it was from another woman," Mrs. Ivins managed with great pain. "He was silent a long time. She demanded to know if it was true, like the letter said, that he was in love with someone else. He asked if that was why she had left a message for him at work that she had to talk to him. She said yes. He said, 'You made me take off from work and find you here so you could ask me a question like that?'"

Mrs. Ivins sat slumped in the chair. "He wouldn't deny it," she said. "He apparently couldn't. I don't know what came over me. If you had asked me earlier today who was my prize pupil in fifty years here, I would have said Tom Noel." She began to weep softly. "That boy was the most interested, most spiritually sensitive child I have ever seen. To see him turn his back on all that he learned, on all that he knows, on all that he's built over the years, well, I just couldn't take it."

"What happened?" Grew probed.

"Well, he finally asked her what if it was true, what if it was the only way to get back at her for doing the same thing to him."

Roger was stunned. He knew infidelity was rampant, even

among believers, but he had never known anything about discord in the Noel family.

"Can you imagine?" the old woman said. "She had been unfaithful to him, too."

"Pardon me for asking such an indelicate question, ma'am," the cop said, "but why didn't you kill her too?"

"I might have if I hadn't come to my senses," she said. "Tom's wife had left when I came out and surprised him. I might have gone after her too, but when I realized what I had done to him, I knew I was in real trouble."

"You surprised him?" Grew pursued.

The woman nodded. "I waited, listening to see if they would say anything more. She said something about her crime—or something like that—being ten years ago. He said he had never got over it. They didn't say anything for a minute or so, and I didn't realize she had left. I came out of that washroom not knowing what I would do. He had his back to me and was heading into the men's room across the hall. I found myself just running at him, crashing into him from behind. His head hit that door and I pushed him all the way into the bathroom and tackled him. His head hit one of the stalls, I think, and then the floor. I was a little dazed myself. By the time I tried to help him, he was gasping for breath and his head was bleeding."

Hollis Grew glanced briefly at Roger, then turned back to Mrs. Ivins. "His head was bleeding?"

Her voice broke. "Yes. It was awful, horrible. And to think I did it."

"So that was how he died, ma'am?"

She nodded miserably.

"You used no weapon? You did nothing else to him but ram him as he entered the washroom?"

She shook her head and dabbed at her eyes.

"Ma'am, that's all I need. I appreciate your cooperation. You are free to go."

Dorcas Ivins looked up, startled. "Excuse me? I just killed a man and—"

"Mrs. Ivins, you did not kill Mr. Noel. He was mortally wounded before you touched him, and his head hitting the door or the wall or the floor was not serious enough to kill him."

"Then how—?"

"I'm afraid I can't tell you that just now. The one who did it is the one who knows, and we don't want word getting out about the details until we complete our investigation."

The woman sat shaking her head. "You're sure I didn't kill him? I wanted to. Surely I hurt him. I feel terrible about all of this."

"Ma'am, Tom Noel was over six feet tall and weighed more than two hundred pounds. Didn't it surprise you that you could knock him over so easily?"

"I thought I had caught him off guard."

Grew seemed to be fighting a smile. He stood and gently touched Mrs. Ivins's shoulder. "Can your friend here help you get cleaned up and see you home?"

"Of course," Mrs. Grom said. "But sir, I believe you owe this lady an apology."

Grew hesitated. "You understand my situation. I have an ugly murder here and a woman who was found with the victim and who is ready to confess. I had to arrest her and read her her rights in case her confession was real. I wouldn't have wanted to lose her on a technicality."

"But she was mistaken."

"Of course she was. Or covering for someone—which I don't believe either, so don't give me that look." He turned back to Mrs. Ivins. "I can apologize to you, ma'am, for what you've had to go through, but I'd be lying if I said I'd have done it any other way."

By now the old woman was standing and trying to steady herself. The detective held her elbow as Marjorie helped her to the door. "You know what?" Dorcas said, turning slightly to face him. "You ought to start coming to Sunday school!"

When the women were gone, Hollis Grew said, "My people are already at the Noel home, of course. I need to call and tell them the wife has become a prime suspect."

When the detective was finished on the phone, he told Roger, "You realize this puts you in a tenuous situation, too, don't you, sir?"

"Because I know as well as you do that there was a murder weapon, and I even know what it was?"

The detective nodded. "Would *you* like a lawyer?"

"Call me reckless," Roger said, "but I've never been convinced that innocent people need lawyers."

"You thought Mrs. Ivins needed one."

"Touché. Anyway, she can vouch for the fact that I heard her screaming and found her with Tom."

"And who can vouch for where you were a couple of minutes earlier when someone punctured him twice?"

Roger was silent. Who could? He wanted to remind himself of all the people who had been in his office that day, and whether he had stepped away long enough to give them an opportunity to walk off with those scissors. But why would anyone plan a murder and grab a weapon as an afterthought, clearly trying to implicate Roger in the process?

The detective continued. "We're going to need to fingerprint you, Mr. Rhodes."

Roger shrugged. "You're going to find my prints on the bathroom door and on several surfaces in there."

"The question is whether we'll find them on the murder weapon."

"I wasn't stupid enough to touch that, if that's what you mean."

"That's not what I mean, and that was a non-denial denial. Were you aware of that?"

"I'm a psychologist," Roger said, thinking that if a parishioner of his was not in the morgue right then, he might have even smiled. "I'm an observer of evasion."

"And you're evading me. I ask you again: do you need legal counsel? Do I need to arrest you and read you your rights?"

"Do what you have to do," Roger said, "but I will tell you all I know regardless."

"Are you sure you want to?"

"Of course."

Roger told him of his daughter's visit and of his having handled the scissors before they became the murder weapon. Roger opened the drawer and Grew leaned over to look. When Roger reached for the case, Grew grabbed his wrist. "We'll want to dust that, especially if you're sure someone else touched it."

"Someone had to."

"If you're telling me the truth," Grew said, "your prints on the scissors may have been obliterated by blood or the hands of the killer."

"Or maybe not."

"True enough," the cop said. "Modern forensics is a marvel."

"I will submit to a lie detector test."

"Those are still inadmissible," Grew said.

"Anyway, you don't have a motive for me."

"That sounds like a guilty man talking."

"Sorry. It just seems I would have needed a reason."

"Maybe you're Mrs. Noel's guy from ten years ago, hm?"

Roger snorted. "I'm the most committed husband you know."

"That wouldn't be saying much. Listen, do you have an idea who was in your office today? Any way Mrs. Noel could have been?"

Roger shook his head. "Not to my knowledge." He pored over his schedule and ticked off his various appointments, his heart thumping when he saw names here and there with loose connections to the Noel family. He began to suspect everybody. Two of the women he had counseled that day had had affairs with men whose names they had not revealed yet, but both claimed they were in the past. Roger didn't know what to tell Grew. There was counselor-client privilege. There was also his own neck to protect. Truth and time, he had always believed, walk hand in hand.

As Roger rehashed in his mind any unusual circumstances about his appointments that day, he ran out of ideas. If he had left someone in his office briefly, which wasn't unusual, he didn't recall who or when or why.

"Let me tell you my problem," Grew said, pulling a pack of cigarettes from his pocket.

"Sorry, we'll have to step outside for that," Roger said.

They walked down the hall, past the washrooms, which were cordoned off with yellow tape and still had police personnel combing every inch. "The lab is transmitting some of the dusting to D.C. now," another detective whispered to Grew.

Hollis stopped and ran a hand through his hair, the unlit cigarette still in his fingers. "Do me a favor, Rhodes. If you're clean you've got nothing to worry about, so how about letting my guys print you right here, save me a warrant, save you a trip to the station, all that. We can have your prints to the FBI within a half hour, and you can know where you stand."

"I already know where I stand," Roger said. "But sure, I'm easy."

While Grew stepped outside for his smoke, a technician pulled a portable fingerprinting kit from a black leather attaché. Though no one in the building knew him, Roger felt conspicuous as the stranger rolled each finger and thumb through the ink and onto the cards. "You gonna shoot a mug shot here too?" Roger said, smiling.

"We could," the tech said. "But you're not being booked. You're just being cooperative." He paused. "You snuff this guy, or what?"

Was this a test? A setup? Surely Grew knew he couldn't smoke in the church. Had the whole charade been intended to get Roger to this point, where he could be intimidated and feel guilty? Was the nice-guy Grew making room for a tough-guy approach, a new face trying to get him to confess? Roger was angry, but he would not lose control. He was a psychologist who could just as easily use emotion as detect it. He turned the tables on the technician.

"I happen to be the dead man's pastor," he said. "Right now I'm nearly overcome with shock and grief, if you don't mind."

The man looked down. "Sorry. I was just curious."

He gave Roger a moist cloth to wipe the ink from his hands, then stepped down to the door where he let Grew in. The detective's cigarette was still unlit, and Roger noticed the technician shake his head slightly. *Nice try,* Roger thought.

"Step outside with me," Grew said. In the cool night air Roger's breath looked only slightly less dense than the smoke Grew finally produced. "I gotta tell you something. Your only alibi is a little old lady who may be sharp for her age, but she's sadly mistaken and not very convincing. I mean, she's a wisp of a woman who could have killed herself doing what she says she did. You gotta do better than such a weak witness. The only guy who can corroborate her story is not gonna be telling anybody anything. Even though you've got the scissors case in your office and we're gonna find your prints on the scissors, you're sticking with saying that you came upon the scene after it had all gone down?"

Roger nodded resignedly.

"I may have to arrest you, sir."

"Yeah, maybe. Could I call my wife? I'm sure she's heard by now and is frantic to hear from me."

They walked back in where a uniformed policeman carrying a mobile phone informed Grew that Mrs. Noel admitted having the argument but said that when she stormed off her husband was fine. She was looking for her daughter who was to drive her home.

"Maybe the daughter overheard the argument, just like Mrs. Ivins did," Grew said. "Check her out, too. And get prints on both of them."

When Roger and Hollis Grew reached his office again, the answering machine was blinking. Roger pushed the button to hear the voice of his wife.

"Call me, honey. The kids are in bed, and I can't get a baby-sitter. I figured I shouldn't come over there anyway. I can't believe the news. Are you all right? Suzie is still awake and crying. I haven't told her anything, but she's frantic to talk to you. She says she has to tell you something. I hope you're on your way home."

Roger turned to Grew, as if to ask what he should do. Grew cocked his head. "You can tell your wife whatever you want, but what I'd like is for you to wait until I hear whether your prints are on those scissors. If they are, you've got a big job ahead of you."

"Clearing myself, you mean?"

"Whatever."

For the first time, Roger began to fear for his freedom, his career, his reputation, his family, his future. Was it possible he could go to prison for something he didn't do? He called his wife, deciding to not worry her with the news until and unless he was arrested.

"I'm helping the police right now," he told her. "It may be some time before I'm home, so don't wait up. I'll call you if it's going to be after midnight. . . . She's still awake? Sure, I'll talk to her, but, hon, it's nine-thirty. . . . Well, if she's that upset.

"Hi, Suzie. What's the trouble? You want to talk to me about the scissors?"

Grew leaped from his chair and hit the speaker button on Roger's phone.

"What about them, sweetie?"

"I'm sorry, Daddy! I disobeyed you."

"What do you mean?"

"Will you be mad? I don't want a spanking."

"Tell me, Suzie. What do you mean?"

"When you were talking to the secretary lady I got the scissors out of the case from your desk and took them with me."

"You took them to school? Do you still have them?"

"No," she said, crying. "I started feeling real bad, but I didn't want to take them back to you, so I just dropped them."

"You dropped them?"

"Well, threw them I guess."

"Where, honey? Do you remember? It's real important."

"Down by the bathroom I just kinda tossed them, and I think they bounced off the top of the coatrack and landed on that furnace thing."

"Furnace thing?"

"You know, Daddy. Where you turn on the furnace. They were still showing, and I was afraid you would see them, but they were up too high and I couldn't reach them so I just left them. I've felt awful all day."

"I forgive you, honey. Thanks for telling me. You know you felt bad because what you did was wrong."

"Uh-huh. Am I going to get a spanking?"

"Did you tell Jesus you were sorry?"

"About twenty times!"

"I don't think you need a spanking this time."

Grew was standing, fidgeting. When Roger said good night to his daughter, Grew said, "Show me."

They strode quickly down the hall. Just before the bathrooms and the foyer they came upon a built-in coatrack recessed into the wall.

"Is this the furnace thing?" Grew said, pointing to a thermostat.

Roger nodded, his eyes widening. Grew called down the hall, and a uniformed officer tossed him a flashlight. He crouched until his eyes were level with the top of the tiny thermostat. He shined the light horizontally. "This could be your lucky day, Rhodes," he said. "This thing hasn't been dusted for a while. Look here, but don't touch."

Roger eyeballed the top of the tiny box in the beam of light. The thin layer of dust had been recently disturbed, as if someone had taken something on his way past. The scissors were nowhere in sight.

"Techie!" Grew shouted, and the print man hurried over. The detective pointed to the top of the box, and the officer went to work.

Just over an hour later, Roger Rhodes drove home alone with a story his wife would find hard to believe. A clear middle fingerprint atop the thermostat and a clear enough thumbprint from one thin edge of the scissors belonged to Parke Noel. Her mother had, as she had said, bristled away from her husband. But as he stood there watching her retreat, Parke appeared from the dark foyer where she, like Mrs. Ivins, had overheard. She hurried after her mother, then whirled in a rage, the scissors catching her eye. He probably hadn't even seen her reach up and snatch them off the thermostat.

She marched back to him and plunged them into his neck, ripping a gash in his carotid artery. When he had spun away from her and grabbed his neck, she plunged the scissors into a lung from the back. As he staggered toward the bathroom, she ran down the hall. It was then that Mrs. Ivins emerged, crashing into Tom in the dimly lit foyer and pushing him through the bathroom door, sending the scissors flying.

Parke Noel fled to the car where she was able to compose herself and avoid suspicion, hiding the fact that she had overheard. In the most horrible irony of all, a note from Tom's "mistress" arrived the next day, apologizing for a joke carried too far. The woman had been put up to the trick by a friend of Tom's. She and Tom had never met.

Two weeks later, with the church still in shock, a subdued celebration of Dorcas Ivins's fifty years of service saw Roger Rhodes bring a brief devotional. Many of Mrs. Ivins's past and present students were there, including Suzie Rhodes.

THE TANGLED
WEB

Elizabeth Grissom's father was not wealthy, but there was an air about him. How can it be delicately put? Douglas thought people were more interested in him than was the case. When he sensed attention waning, he resorted to stretching the truth.

For instance, a particularly heinous murder once rocked the employees at the office where Douglas worked in mid-management (which he always represented as "top" or "high-level" management). The victim was a middle-aged cleaning lady whom Douglas had greeted every few days for several years. She worked for a service and thus was not part of the full-time staff where Douglas was a systems analyst.

Yet when it came time to testify one night at First Church, he rose to tearfully reveal that the unfortunate deceased—mur-

dered by an escapee from a hospital for the criminally insane
—was a dear colleague. No one in the church could have
known the difference, so as Douglas stood there looking appropriately saddened and shocked, groans of sympathy emanated
from the congregation. He also allowed that though he was reluctant to reveal it because he might jeopardize any heavenly
reward, he had, in fact, just about earned the right to be heard
by the now departed one. A dire warning and reminder to re-
deem the time to share one's faith.

Elizabeth, the Grissoms' wide-eyed and freckled college
sophomore, was home on semester break. She caught the eyes
of her brother, Cameron, a lanky high school senior, and they
tried to hide their frowns. "If she was such a dear friend," Cameron asked Elizabeth later, "how come her name was never
mentioned in our house? I'm surprised Dad didn't recall a
strange man stalking her just the other day."

Douglas Grissom, you see, capitalized even on bloody
mayhem for a brief season of borrowed fame. Once he tried to
put a positive spin on the misfortune of a beautiful young woman who had, in the prime of her teen years, been the victim of
an accident in which she became a quadriplegic. She had since
become a nationally known speaker, a singer, and a Christian
television personality. "If it hadn't been for that accident, she
never would have become so well-known."

Liz had shot her father a double take. "You're saying it was
worth it? That she would have chosen that horrible handicap?"

"I believe she would have," he intoned.

Liz said no more. She intended her question to challenge
her father; he had taken it as interest. She shook her head as
she told her brother, "Cam, the man would be willing to break
his neck and live in a wheelchair just to be known."

When Douglas had overcome the loss of his "friend," he

testified of his gratefulness that he had been so mightily used by the Lord among his coworkers. "They were in pain." Elizabeth thought her father's gratitude tended to make his own availability and sensitivity as important as anything God did, but that was his way. Every time he talked about his wife or his children, he feigned embarrassment and surprise over their accomplishments.

A letter from Cameron to Elizabeth, shortly after she returned to college, evidenced the extent of the problem:

Dear Liz,

What you're doing there, as you can imagine, is nothing compared to how Dad represents it. You said you didn't make the choir because they had enough altos so you became an alternate with the women's glee club, right? Dad tells people you were selected for the women's ensemble because of your trained voice. I said, "Women's glee, Dad," but it was in front of someone so I got that cold look before he smiled and said, "Yes, the women's glee ensemble." Of course, I heard about it later for correcting him. He said, "You made me sound like a liar." I wanted to say, "Bingo!"

What gets to me is the injustice of it. People who don't live with him can't tell the difference. If I went around straightening out every tall tale Dad told, I'd look terrible and so would he. Not to mention that I wouldn't have time for anything else.

I tried out for basketball, you know. I didn't really want to, but Mom told me it would "mean a lot to your father." I wanted to say, "If it means so much to him, why doesn't *he* go out?" We're supposed to honor our parents and love and obey them because that's what God wants. Well, He wants truth too. How does that add up?

Anyway, almost fifty guys came out for the varsity. I hadn't played since I was a freshman—and then I was a bench sitter on the B team. Remember, they didn't cut anybody. We all sat there in those huge, hand-me-down uniforms, trying to keep the straps up on our shoulders, and we runts played only the last thirty seconds of lost causes. Liz, I love the game, but I don't even start on the church team.

I'm bigger now, and I was hoping maybe I would somehow get picked. But I was one of the slowest guys and most inept jumpers, so I had no chance.

One of the coaches said he liked the way I hustled, because I chased a loose ball while I was supposed to be waiting to shoot free throws. I didn't mind trying out, but I was wasting their time. They thanked me for trying, and I got cut with about two dozen other guys after the first night. Another couple of dozen were gone by the end of the week, so no big deal. I see some of them around, and we kid each other about how we were overlooked.

Are you ready for how Dad tells it? He says I was cut at the last minute and that he has it on good authority that I was the thirteenth man on a twelve-man squad, the last to be cut. He even adds a few more embellishments, like how it must have pained the coach to let me go. Of course the next time he tells it, the coach has actually said that.

I'd like to expose Dad, I really would. Meanwhile, I know you'll destroy this letter. I miss you.

Love, Cam

Why neither Elizabeth nor her brother had let their disgust bubble over into rebellion could be attributed to their concern for their too-patient mother and to Elizabeth's getting serious about her faith.

She had been on the edge of wildness in her mid-teens. Then she went to a church teen retreat and saw God work among her friends. She heard them pray for her. Elizabeth realized she could no more live with an inherited faith than she could accept as hereditary the values of her father. A wise counselor listened as she spilled her story. Elizabeth carefully avoided using the word *lying* to describe her father's actions. The counselor, a college senior named Beverly, heard her try to excuse him, but Beverly would not let it go.

"It's lying, Elizabeth, and the sooner you face that and deal with it, the better chance you'll have to avoid falling into the same trap."

There was, however, a part of Beverly's advice that Elizabeth chose to ignore. Although she got her own spiritual life in order as it hadn't been since she was a kid, she never confronted her father. And his lying grew worse. She had been thrilled to go off to college, not realizing that that gave her father only more ammunition.

When Douglas came home with the news that his company was sending him to Switzerland over spring break and that he planned to take the family, not even Elizabeth's mother believed him. "You hardly ever travel," Nancy Grissom countered.

"The president himself asked me to be his emissary," he said, looking wounded. "I'm honored, and I'm eager to serve in this strategic role."

The assignment memo told a different story. It was from the president of the company and was addressed to the executive vice president, Douglas's boss's boss's boss. It read: "Earl, I've been asked by corporate to go to Switzerland again to accept that crazy humanitarian award for the chairman of the board. They said I could delegate it, so that's what I'm doing. Don't feel obligated to do it yourself. Believe me, it's no picnic, unless picnics bore you. Why not give it to someone who would be thrilled. Thanks, Earl. I owe you one."

The memo had gone from the president to the executive vice president to the vice president to the manager and then to the area supervisor where Douglas worked. It had notes all over it: "Huh-uh," "No way!" "Not me!" and "Thanks a lot!"

Elizabeth couldn't help but laugh at a note from one of Dad's coworkers: "I'd really love to see Switzerland, but we have a wedding we can't miss in the spring. Try Grissom. He'd eat this up."

To get the money to take the family, Douglas borrowed some and sold Nancy's car. "Whatever it takes," Cameron told Elizabeth. "Can you imagine the mileage he'll get from this?"

By the time the story reached First Church, Douglas revealed that he had been praying for just this sort of an opportunity to minister overseas. This assignment, direct to Douglas from the chairman of the board, was an answer to prayer.

Pastor Nigel Ingle congratulated Douglas and mentioned that an old seminary acquaintance of his was in Switzerland. "I understand he's on sabbatical from his own church and serves as interim pastor in the Swiss foothills of the Austrian Alps."

"I'll look him up," Douglas said. "We expect to encourage fellow believers."

"I haven't spoken with him for years," the pastor said, "but if you get close, you might greet him for me."

"Being overseas might be the perfect opportunity to confront Dad," Elizabeth told her mother.

"After all these years?" Nancy complained. "It's too late, Liz."

All the way overseas Elizabeth plotted her strategy. Her biggest fear, of course, was how her father would react.

"At worst he could disown me," Elizabeth told her brother.

"I thought you said at worst," Cameron said.

"Cam!"

The family spent a night in Frankfurt, then headed south into Switzerland by train the next morning. Jet lag had taken its toll. Tempers were short, and Elizabeth was losing her resolve. "What can possibly come of it?" she whispered.

"Don't chicken out on me now, Liz," Cameron said. "I'm counting on you."

"Oh, good! *You're* counting on *me*. Where have you been all these years? You feed me stories, but have you ever called his bluff?"

"Have you, Liz?"

"I've tried."

"Like when?"

"I don't remember."

"How many times?"

"Not enough."

"See? You're going to back out," he said. "I can see it coming."

"You backed out long ago," she said. "So don't start with me."

By the time the family reached the Swiss side of the Austrian Alps, Douglas was in such a good mood that Elizabeth almost forgot the imminent crisis. Apparently her father saw no need to exaggerate anything in the midst of such beauty. Postcards did no justice to the panorama of color.

Elizabeth's mother found a tiny shop on a side street where she purchased hard salami sandwiches with cheese on dark bread and a jug of aged, carbonated apple juice. The family had skipped breakfast and now carried their lunch into the foothills, finding their breathing more labored the higher they trekked into the Alps. The day was clear and crisp, and patches of snow dotted the way until they were high enough to find it covering the ground.

All they wanted was to sit and eat. How could any lunch have ever tasted as good as those fresh, pungent sandwiches in that brisk, pure air?

The time was right, and Elizabeth knew it.

"Dad," she began, so solemnly that he stopped chewing and stared first at Nancy and then at Elizabeth, "I need to talk to you about something serious. I don't want you to interrupt or get defensive, even though this will hurt you. OK?"

"Well," her father began, "what are you—?"

"That's what I mean, Daddy. I don't want you to speak or even react until I'm done. Is that too much to ask?"

"It might be. Let's remember who is the parent and who—"

"Doug," Nancy said, touching him. "That's not too much to ask." Elizabeth could see that her mother was scared.

"First of all," Elizabeth said, "I'm not pregnant." Her father was not amused. "And neither Cam nor I is about to give up our faith. Well, Cameron might."

"That's not funny," her father said, his face reddening.

"Daddy! I'm kidding!"

"Douglas, let her speak," Nancy said.

Douglas looked at his watch and looked away, as if refusing to pay attention. "Daddy," Elizabeth said, "you have time to listen to me."

"I need a nap," he said. "I still have jet lag."

Cameron snorted.

"Well, I do," Douglas said. "Get on with this."

"It won't rush," Elizabeth said, "and I've been thinking about it for too long for you to ignore me. You can do with it what you want. But you are going to hear me."

"You're telling me what I'm going to do?" Douglas said. It was a side of him Elizabeth had not seen. Here she had finally gotten his attention and mustered her courage, and before she even got to her charges, she had chipped loose some deep-seated defensiveness. It was as if he had a premonition that she was onto something far below the surface, and he desperately wanted to keep her at bay. But she was nearly twenty-one years old. She would not be dissuaded.

"If you won't listen to me, Daddy, I will not be going back with you."

"You what?"

Even Cameron was surprised. "What'll you do?" he said.

"I have my own money, and I will consider myself on my own."

Douglas stood.

"Douglas!" Nancy said. "Sit down and listen!" She had begun to weep. "Whatever is that important to her is something you have to listen to."

Douglas looked embarrassed. The man with the perfect, tight-knit, spiritual family of church leaders had discovered himself angry at his older child and scrapping to keep her from anything painful. Willingly or not, he was going to hear this. He sat on a huge rock, folded his arms across his chest, and looked at her with a cocked head.

Elizabeth knew she could keep his attention, because she was not merely prepared to state her case; she was also prepared to begin with her conclusions. When he heard how dire she considered the consequences of his actions, he would have to deal with the issue.

"Daddy," she began slowly, "it's a wonder Cameron and I are even Christians."

Her father looked stricken and began to speak. This time it was Cameron who shut the door. "Dad, for once in your life, let someone else say something, will you?"

"Cameron!" the man said, his throat constricted.

"Just do it, will you Dad?" Cameron said. "Hassle me later, ground me if you want, but just be quiet and listen now, please!"

Nancy touched Douglas's knee. He wrenched away, but he was quiet. Elizabeth, silently praying for strength, felt her heartbeat rock her body. This was the most painful experience of her life, but it had to be done. How many times had she run it over in her mind, reminding herself not to pull punches, not to excuse, not to rationalize? The easy thing to say, if anything about this could be easy, would be, "I know you don't mean to," or, "I'm sure you're not aware of it," or, "There must be some explanation for this." No, she had to jump in with both feet.

"Dad," she said, "over the years Cam and I have seen you, as a regular practice, stretch the truth to the point of lying."

"What?" her father said, rasping in rage. "I never lie."

"This is hard enough as it is, Dad. Now let me finish."

"Just a minute," Cameron broke in. "Dad, you're gonna sit there and say you never lie? Wasn't it you who told the waitress in the pizza place last week that we'd just got those coupons in the mail the day before? They were a month expired, and Mom had dug them out of the junk drawer in the kitchen."

"When was that?"

"Sunday night after church!"

"Oh, Cam," Douglas said, "there's no way they would know the difference."

"So that makes it right?"

"Our witness can't be questioned if they never know," Douglas said, his look betraying that his logic sounded lame even to himself.

"It was a lie, Dad," Cameron said.

"They want you to use those coupons!" Douglas insisted. "They run specials all the time."

"Then why not just ask them, instead of lying?"

"Aah!"

Douglas waved his son off with derision, but his wife's eyes were filling.

"That's not the least of it, Dad," Elizabeth said. "I'm telling you that every day in just about everything you say, you add some twist to make it better."

While Douglas Grissom sat there looking stunned, Elizabeth ticked off a litany of stories from years before all the way to the present, including the embellishments and misrepresentations about Cam's basketball tryouts, her selection to the women's glee club, the relationship between her father and the murdered woman at work, and especially the very trip they were on.

The result was worse than Elizabeth feared, but not as bad as it could have been. There was no violence, no shouting, no irrational behavior. Both parents fell deathly silent, but her father glared at her, clearly seething. She knew she had exposed him for what he was.

Her mother looked neither at Elizabeth nor at Douglas. The four silently packed their stuff and made their way slowly down the mountain trails to the foothills, to the warmer temperatures and the beautiful little village. When Elizabeth got close to her mother on the path, Nancy did not acknowledge her. When Elizabeth quietly addressed her, Nancy merely shook her head slightly, as if to say, "No, not right now, I'm not ready." Elizabeth knew her mother had many things to say, but not in front of her father.

Douglas had always had a flair for sarcasm, and Elizabeth expected a barrage. But when they got back to the inn, he was docile, almost conciliatory. He said he wanted to call on the friend of Pastor Ingle's and that anyone who cared to go with him was welcome. Elizabeth expected at least some sort of a barb, such as, "If anyone can stand hanging around with a liar."

But no. He still appeared hurt. He hadn't seem to repent of any anger. And he certainly did not acknowledge any truth in Elizabeth's charges. She did not mistake his silence for guilt. Sadly, she assumed, a lifetime of misrepresentation had seared lying onto his brain. No one, she believed, was more deceived by Douglas Grissom than he was.

He was back in form an hour later as the family was welcomed into a beautiful chalet. Dr. Harold Green and his wife, Grace, were pleased to see people from the States and gave the family a tour of the parsonage with its stunning view. When they were seated, Douglas grew ebullient.

"You and my pastor must have been very close," he began.

"And your pastor is?"

"Nigel Ingle from First Suburban in—"

Dr. Green quickly glanced at his wife. "Well, not really. Actually—"

"He mentions you frequently from the pulpit."

"He does?"

"Some tidbit of collegiate or seminary wisdom you imparted, some example you were to his spiritual life. It's always something."

"That's strange, because—"

"Well, he's a generous man that way, take it from one who really knows him. He's tossed bouquets my way that I don't really deserve, but they're still encouraging."

"Well, I can't imagine he—"

"All I know is, he considers you a cherished friend, someone very special from his past."

"I—"

"He wanted me to personally greet you and pass along the best wishes of our church, and to see if there was anything the body of believers here needs that we could help provide."

"He did?"

"Absolutely."

Interim Pastor Green leaned forward. "The fact is, this church has a dire need for the equivalent of about ten thousand American dollars. They have a debt that has to be paid so they can keep their building. We have been praying about it, and frankly we were hoping that an individual would underwrite it. If a Stateside church could help us with that, we'd be grateful. It would have to be a gift, and it would have to happen soon. I wouldn't even have suggested such a thing, but since you asked, I thought maybe the Lord was in it."

"Not only is the Lord in it, brother, but I am authorized to commit to it."

"You are?"

"I've been in leadership at First Suburban for many, many years. If there's any hesitation on their part, I will personally make up the difference, up to the entire amount. How soon do you need it?"

"You don't want to know."

"I certainly do."

"In about ten days."

"We will still be in Switzerland, so perhaps the funds could be wired to us. I'll tell you what. I'll arrange with my bank to have the money transferred here from one of my credit cards, then I will have the church reimburse me when we get back."

"But what if they don't want—"

"Then I'll just consider it a personal gift."

Dr. Green fought tears as he reached for the benefactor from America. He stood and prayed, thanking God for answered prayer in the form of this wonderful, selfless, giving man and his family. "God will reward you," he said.

Elizabeth admired her mother for saying nothing until they got back to the inn. There she took Douglas into the tiny sitting room off the bedroom where she apparently thought Elizabeth and Cameron could not hear.

"Douglas," she began, "what in the world were you thinking? Elizabeth was right! You have such a need to promote yourself that you've made a promise that will sink us. Our credit cards are at their limits. There's no way the church will make a decision that quickly, and even if they did, they won't see the need to wire money here that fast.

"It's obvious Pastor Ingle and this man hardly knew each other. And you, pretending to be a close friend of Pastor Ingle and a leader in the church! You call ushering being a leader for many years? I've been troubled for years by things you've said, and I should have confronted you. How could you do that to-day, after what Liz said this morning? Douglas, you lied. I've never heard Pastor mention Dr. Green's name. Did you see the name of that church? It's a state church, a liturgical church. It may be perfectly fine, but no one at First Church is going to be comfortable supporting it without knowing more. And even if they did, you had no right! Why, Douglas? Why do you feel the need to do this?"

There was long silence from the sitting room. Elizabeth and Cameron edged closer. Could it be their father was speech-less for once? That he felt bad? They had never seen him cry. Was that next?

"You don't know what it's like," he whined, "to grow up in poverty."

"Douglas, I've known you since first grade, and your family wasn't any worse off than mine."

"I don't know how many times I heard, 'We can't afford it.' If it was once it was several times a day."

"That was true in my family too, honey. Even for necessi-ties my dad used to always say, 'Wait till payday and see how much we have left.'"

"Well, Nancy, I hated that. I was invisible, a nobody, a poor, never-have-anything kid."

"And now you're somebody?"

"Some people think I am."

"But you're not, Doug! Your whole reputation is built on lies."

"Lies? Embellishments, maybe, but—"

"Douglas, you make up stories. You need help! We come from the same town, the same background, the same economic level. You can't blame this on your upbringing. You've got such a need to be somebody that you have created your own world. It doesn't exist."

"How can you say that?"

"Because I love you."

"What if I promise to never—"

"Douglas! This isn't some *thing* you can undo. It isn't about turning over a new leaf. It isn't just lying; it's how a Christian could do that without a conscience problem."

"OK, OK, I see it. All right?"

"No! It's so subtle, so insidious that even I had become callused to it. It's wrong. It's sin. But it's deep, don't you see?"

She had pushed him too far. "No!" he shouted. "No, I don't! You're making a big thing out of nothing! So I exaggerate once in a while. It doesn't hurt anybody. I told that guy I would get him the ten thousand, and I will. If you don't want me to tell the church or the pastor, fine."

"Sure, and make him think the church turned him down."

"He doesn't care where the money comes from! I'll cut corners. We'll dig out. And I won't do this again, I promise."

"Douglas, we're going to have enough trouble digging out from this trip! You need to extricate yourself from this with the truth."

"I'm supposed to tell Green I lied to him?"

"That would be the only right thing to do."

Douglas didn't respond for several seconds. "I have my self-righteous daughter to thank for this," he spat.

"I wouldn't call her self-righteous," Nancy said. "But otherwise you're right, and I'm proud of her. She has somehow survived the mess you've created. I share the blame, Douglas, and the only way we're going to move on from here is to get to the bottom of it."

"There's nothing to get to the bottom of! So I got a little off track. I know now, OK? I know. You don't think I can change; you watch."

Nancy had heard enough. She left the sitting room and slammed the door, collapsing in tears on the bed. Cameron, embarrassed, left the room. Elizabeth sat next to her mother and stroked her back.

"He'll never change," Nancy sobbed. "It's too deep, too embedded."

"You did the right thing, Mom."

"So did you, Liz! How long have you been holding that in?"

"Too long."

Her mother sat up and looked at her. "How long?"

"Probably since junior high, when I found myself doing it too."

Her mother buried her face in her hands. "I don't think he's going to make it right with Dr. Green either. I know him. Too much pride. You may have opened some sliver of hope that he'll get help, but it'll be a long, painful process. I'm just sorry you kids had to suffer. That's my fault. I should have done years ago what you did this morning."

"But it didn't work."

"Something's happening, Liz. It may not turn out the way we want it to, and it may make our lives worse for a while, but what you said was right, and what you did was good."

Douglas came out of the sitting room in a quiet rage, glaring at his wife and his daughter. "I need to call my bank," he said.

"Oh, Douglas, no," Nancy said. "Let's talk to Dr. Green."

"And admit I was lying, is that what you're saying? And then I don't follow through on my commitment besides? No way! I'm going to find the money and get it here, like I said I would. I'm going to be a man of my word."

Nancy rose from the bed and tried to touch her husband, but his look stopped her as she drew near. "Honey, I want you to be a man of your word, but that means admitting what you've done."

But he stormed out. Nancy turned to embrace her daughter. "Liz, someone needs to go to Dr. Green. Would you?"

"What about Daddy calling his bank?"

"He's bluffing."

"How do you know?"

"He's not stupid. No banks are open at this time in the States. I'll hang around here with Cam in case your father comes back."

Dr. Green welcomed Elizabeth with a knowing, sympathetic look. "I'm so glad you returned," he said. "I need to talk to your father. My wife told me after you left that I came on too strong with my request, and we fear Mr. Grissom felt obligated to do more than he was able."

"That's what I wanted to talk to you about," Elizabeth said. "We—"

"I should tell you that I called your pastor after you left. It was very late there, but he was gracious. As I suspected, he told me candidly that it would be unlikely his church would act quickly on such a request and that he doubted the figure would be anywhere close to half of the ten thousand."

"Did he also tell you that my dad is not in a position to obligate the church?"

Dr. Green hung his head. "Yes," he said. "He did."

"Did he also tell you that Daddy is not in a position to make up the difference?"

"Yes, I'm afraid he told me that too. He warned me to take much of what Mr. Grissom says with a grain of salt."

Elizabeth was stricken by the realization that if Pastor Ingle knew that, then many, many others must too. It broke her heart.

"I'm sorry," she said. "And I'm embarrassed."

"Miss Grissom, do you mind if I speak frankly?

"Please."

"I need to tell you that you should be more than sorry and embarrassed, though I can certainly understand those emotions. Don't be sorry for any inconvenience on my part. At my wife's urging, I told no one of your father's generous, and—as it turns out—unwise offer. But I do think you have cause to worry."

"I *am* worried."

"I sense this is a pattern with your father, and—"

"Yes."

"And Pastor Ingle's impression seems to confirm that."

"Yes."

"Elizabeth, I need to speak with your father. Is he feeling bad?"

"He's committed to honoring his commitment. He was exposed this morning, and he's mad." She told of her own confrontation. Dr. Green was impressed.

"Yet he did this immediately afterward," he said.

She nodded, fighting tears.

"I suppose you know that your father's embellishing and posturing are only symptoms, evidences of the real difficulty."

"That's exactly what Mom told him this afternoon," Elizabeth said.

"You understand then that it's a deep-seated self-esteem malady."

She nodded. "Does this happen to be your area of expertise, Dr. Green?"

"As a matter of fact, it is."

"Are you a psychologist, then?"

"No. My doctorate is in theology. I'm an expert at self-worth problems like this because I am a fellow-sufferer."

Elizabeth didn't know what to say.

"When I was in seminary I had such a low opinion of myself that I was not a nice person. Not only was I obnoxious, but I also got into trouble. I cheated. Don't look so stunned. Yes, it even happens in seminary. It didn't mean I wasn't a Christian. It didn't even necessarily mean that I could never have a ministry. It did, however, require that I be caught, be confronted, confess, repent, and be disciplined. Then I needed counseling for the problem itself. It was a long, hard road back, and I began in my mid-twenties. Your father, I assume, is in his forties."

Elizabeth nodded. "But he's so defensive. I can hardly allow myself to even hope—"

"I was defensive too. I hated everyone involved with my apprehension. I resented their love and caring, and I rejected their efforts to get close to me and help me. It was only after months of God's working in my life that I could look back and see who really cared enough to take the risk of making me face myself. If you and your mother and the boy—"

"Cameron."

"Right, if you three hang in there with your father, he will one day look back on this with gratitude. For you."

Elizabeth had trouble believing that.

Douglas was humiliated to learn that Dr. Green had called his pastor and to know what Nigel Ingle had said. Dr. Green had advised that Elizabeth not tell Douglas about about his own seminary experience. "Let me use that if he chooses to come to me."

For the next several days Douglas was sullen and awkward with the family. Meanwhile, the rest prayed that he would act on his own, that he would seek out Dr. Green. Nancy told Elizabeth she had never before worried about Douglas committing suicide. Now she didn't know what to think. He didn't pray, didn't read his Bible, didn't talk much. The family prayed that God would work on him.

Finally, the day came near the end of their trip when Douglas quietly told his wife, "I owe Dr. Green an apology." Elizabeth held her breath, hoping her mother wouldn't push.

"An apology?" Nancy said.

"For putting him in that position with his old friend."

"Whatever you think."

Later Dr. Green told Elizabeth what had happened that day. "Your father came to me a broken man," he said. "I saw nothing to indicate that he was still trying to snow me. But neither did I see any indication that he knew the depth of his problem. Like all of us who have realized that we are wrong and sinful, he wanted a quick fix. I had none to offer.

"He sat in my living room and wept. I knew how hard the process would be for him because he didn't want to talk about it, didn't want to be specific about any of his lies. I suggested that the problem was his self-image and although I agreed that part of it might stem from his humble upbringing, I did not let him use that as an excuse.

"I told him there were several crucial steps on his road to recovery, and none of them would be pleasant. I don't know whether he is up to the journey or not. He'll have to prove that himself. I told him he needed counseling by someone who knew what he was doing and who cared deeply for him. I recommended your pastor. Your father asked, 'If he cares so deeply for me, why would he say such things behind my back? Why wouldn't he have confronted me?'

"I told him I didn't know but that I suspected Nigel had no idea how deep the problem was. A little surface braggadocio is a long way from pathological lying to the point where you begin to believe your own stories. I tried to impress upon your father how important it was that he dredge up every piece of fiction about himself that he had planted in his own brain, examine it, and tell himself the truth. It will not be easy. Really, he will work hard, but the lasting results will be wrought only by the Spirit of God. I fear I scared him a bit."

"Is he not going to pursue help then?" Elizabeth asked.

"Oh, I think he will. When the time came, I had to pull out my ace, didn't I?"

"Your ace?"

"I told him that he should feel fortunate and not humiliated if his own pastor becomes his counselor. Because his pastor was not my counselor. Nigel Ingle played an entirely different role in my recovery from low self-esteem, lying, and cheating. He was the one who found me out, who caught me and confronted me. When I tried to blow him off, he came back with a witness. Then they reported me. People I considered friends, though I didn't know the meaning of the word, I started calling finks, snitches, squealers.

"To my shame, I kept Nigel Ingle in that category for years. Even when I had made tremendous progress, was allowed back into seminary, was ordained, and began pastoring, I hadn't mended the rift between us. I resented his successes. I resented *him.* I waited far too long to make things right."

"When did you finally reconcile?" Elizabeth asked.

"Your father asked the same thing. I was ashamed to tell

him. I pleaded with him not to make the same mistake. I think I got through to him."

He paused, and Elizabeth realized he had not answered her question. Would she have to hear it from her father? Would her dad even want to talk about his discussion with Dr. Green?

When he spoke again, Harold Green's voice betrayed his emotion. "The fact is," he began slowly, "I harbored animosity in my heart for Nigel Ingle for much too long. When I had dealt with everyone and everything else, I still kept him in an ugly, dark corner of my heart. That seed of bitterness did its poisonous work on my spiritual life until I drifted from the Lord. It affected my marriage, my relationships with my children, with my board, my parishioners. It wasn't overt. Many of them didn't even notice. But I did. I was a vagrant in a barren land. I was dying of spiritual thirst. I pleaded for a sabbatical. Though my church could not afford to pay me or even finance the trip, they allowed me the time. That's why I'm here."

"This was that recent?"

Dr. Green nodded. "If you ever doubt that God has a sense of humor, or that He knows what He's doing, or that He is personally involved in the affairs of men, consider His sending someone from Nigel Ingle's church to find me thousands of miles from home. I came here to deal with my problem, as far from Nigel as I could get. He had written and called many times over the years, and I never responded. One intermediary even pleaded with me to meet with him and with Nigel. I came here to come to grips with that. At first I thought your father was an emissary from Nigel. When I realized he was not, I knew God had met me here. There could be no more running. I had to close that last chapter.

"The conversation and prayer and weeping and laughing Nigel and I enjoyed during that late phone call last week will remain a treasure of my life. I can't wait to get back to see him. I encouraged him to counsel your father himself, though I know he does very little of that.

"I will be praying for both of them and for you and your brother and your mother."

"And I for you," Elizabeth said.

Moody Press, a ministry of the Moody Bible Institute,
is designed for education, evangelization, and edification.
If we may assist you in knowing more about Christ
and the Christian life, please write us without obligation:
Moody Press, c/o MLM, Chicago, Illinois 60610.